Valerie stared at the email... and felt shaken from the inside.

Bethany is such a pretty baby. It would be a shame to have anything happen to her.

"Everything okay?" Trevor asked, coming to stand beside her desk.

She forced the fear from her voice. "Sure. Why?"

"Your hands are shaking." He cupped his hand over hers.

She felt the warmth of his touch, saw the concern in his eyes. Would he think her weak if she revealed her fear? There probably wasn't anything that made this man afraid.

The warmth in his gaze told her to risk sharing. "I just got this."

Trevor's jaw hardened as he looked at the screen. "This is all part of a game. Threatening your kid to upset you."

She let out a shaky breath. "Then it's working."

TEXAS K-9 UNIT:

These lawmen solve the toughest cases with the help of their brave canine partners

Tracking Justice–Shirlee McCoy, January 2013
Detection Mission–Margaret Daley, February 2013
Guard Duty–Sharon Dunn, March 2013
Explosive Secrets–Valerie Hansen, April 2013
Scent of Danger–Terri Reed, May 2013
Lone Star Protector–Lenora Worth, June 2013

Books by Sharon Dunn

Love Inspired Suspense

Dead Ringer
Night Prey
Her Guardian
Broken Trust
Zero Visibility
Guard Duty

SHARON DUNN

has always loved writing, but didn't decide to write for publication until she was expecting her first baby. Pregnancy makes you do crazy things. Three kids, many articles and two mystery series later, she still hasn't found her sanity. Her books have won awards, including a Book of the Year award from American Christian Fiction Writers. She was also a finalist for an *RT Book Reviews* Inspirational Book of the Year award.

Sharon has performed in theater and church productions, has degrees in film production and history and worked for many years as a college tutor and instructor. Despite the fact that her résumé looks as if she couldn't decide what she wanted to be when she grew up, all the education and experience have played a part in helping her write good stories.

When she isn't writing or taking her kids to activities, she reads, plays board games and contemplates organizing her closet. In addition to her three kids, Sharon lives with her husband of twenty-two years, three cats and lots of dust bunnies. You can reach Sharon through her website, www.sharondunnbooks.net.

GUARD DUTY

SHARON DUNN

HARLEQUIN® LOVE INSPIRED® SUSPENSE

Special thanks and acknowledgment to Sharon Dunn for her contribution to the Texas K-9 Unit miniseries.

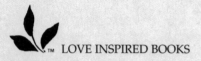

Recycling programs
for this product may
not exist in your area.

LOVE INSPIRED BOOKS

ISBN-13: 978-0-373-18561-0

GUARD DUTY

www.LoveInspiredBooks.com

Printed in U.S.A.

You hear, O Lord, the desire of the afflicted;
you encourage them, and you listen to their cry,
defending the fatherless and the oppressed, in order
that man, who is of the earth, may terrify no more.
—*Psalms* 10:17–18

For Bart, the nervous Border collie,
who has brought laughter
and unconditional devotion into my life.

ONE

"K-9 unit 349. Convenience-store robbery, corner of State and Grand. Suspects are on the run."

As she pushed the talk button to respond to dispatch, rookie officer Valerie Salgado felt that strange mixture of fear and excitement that came every time she responded to a call on patrol.

"Copy. I'm about five blocks from that location. Any idea what direction our perps were going?"

Dispatch responded. "Clerk doesn't know which way they ran. Three males. Two Caucasian, one African American. All dressed in dark clothing."

For the past few months, every call had an extra sense of danger attached to it.

A rash of robberies, drugs and murders that had been escalating in Sagebrush for years had recently been linked to a crime syndicate with an unknown leader.

Valerie hit her siren and sped up.

Maybe this was just a run-of-the-mill robbery, but maybe it was another symptom of a city under siege.

In the back of the patrol car, Valerie's K-9 partner, Lexi, paced from one window to the other, emitting an almost ultrasonic whine. The only one more excited to catch a criminal than Valerie was her two-year-old Rottweiler.

Dispatch came across the line. "Clerk says that two of the men were armed."

Valerie took in a deep breath to calm her nerves. "At least we know what we are dealing with, huh, Lex?"

The dog whined as though she understood.

As she neared the convenience store, Valerie scanned the streets and sidewalks for any sign of movement. Now that it was 10 p.m. and dark, it would be easy enough for the robbers to blend into surroundings if they were smart enough to walk instead of run. Traffic was light, and most of the shops were closed. The all-night burger joint up the street had attracted a little bit of a crowd.

Valerie pulled into the convenience store parking lot. The clerk was easy enough to spot, a distraught fifty-something woman pacing by the store entrance. Valerie got out of her patrol car.

The woman came toward her, eyes wide with fear. The unnatural hair color and heavy makeup revealed rather than hid the woman's age.

The clerk wrapped her arms around herself. Her gaze flitted everywhere. The robbery had shaken the poor woman up. Valerie wanted to hug her and tell her it was going to be all right. But that was not what cops did. Instead, she pulled a notebook out of her utility belt.

She hoped her voice conveyed the level of compassion she felt for what the clerk had just been through. "Ma'am, I'm Officer Salgado. Can you tell me what happened here?"

The woman combed her fingers through her hair. "They took over three hundred dollars. My manager is going to fire me." Her agitated state made her south Texas drawl even more exaggerated.

"How long has it been since the robbers fled the store?"

The clerk closed her eyes as though she were struggling to answer the question. "Umm…they made me lay on the floor facedown." She let out a heavy breath. "I waited until I was sure they weren't going to come back. I…I…called as quickly as I could." She put a trembling hand to her chest. "Maybe five minutes."

Valerie felt torn between desiring to comfort the clerk and wanting to catch the thugs who had terrorized her. Picturing her own mother having to go through something like this made her resolve even stronger. The best comfort she could give this woman would be to see that these perps went to jail.

Valerie glanced up the street. Flashing neon signs for budget hotels stood in contrast to the dark Texas sky. In a pursuit, five minutes was a big lead time.

She cupped the woman's shoulder with her hand, hoping to provide some reassurance. "You go back inside and wait. My dog and I will get these guys."

"Thank you, Officer."

Valerie opened the back door of the patrol car, and Lexi jumped out.

"Get 'em," Valerie commanded, leading the Rottweiler toward the entrance of the convenience store. It would take only minutes for Lexi to pick up on the fear odor that people in flight emitted the second they took off running. Though people couldn't smell it, the scent was extremely distinct to a dog trained to detect it.

Lexi placed her nose to the gravel, trotting in wider and wider circles, returning to the store entrance a couple of times.

Across the street, a dark car with tinted windows came to a stop.

As Lexi worked her way toward

edge of the store parking lot, Valerie glanced at the car. No one got out. The hairs on the back of her neck stood on end as a chill ran over her skin. For weeks now, she had had the sensation of being watched, of eyes pressing on her from dark corners.

The reality of the long arms of the crime syndicate had come home to roost for Valerie. Though she didn't know it at the time, while heading in to the pharmacy a few weeks ago, she'd seen the woman who had most likely murdered Andrew Garry—a local real-estate agent and one of the crime syndicates middle managers. She'd glanced at the woman briefly as she passed her on the dimly lit street out- ide a vacant building by the corner drug- re. Valerie didn't act on her suspicions night, but something about the lady e hooded jacket seemed off. Though ouldn't ID the woman outright, Val- ad the feeling that she would know hen she saw her and that she'd seen mewhere before. It was just a matter of time before something in her brain clicked.

The initial death threat had come the next day only hours after Kip the cadaver dog and his handler had found Garry's body, confirming her suspicions about the woman she'd seen outside the vacant building. Her police email had been hacked into. The threat flashed on her computer screen… *If you testify, you die… maybe even sooner.*

Living with a death threat had become even more complicated. Valerie had recently become guardian to her eighteen-month-old niece, Bethany, after her sister Kathleen's death over two months ago.

The department had offered her protection during her off-duty hours. On duty was a little harder, but she noticed that another patrol car always seemed to be close. Sagebrush P.D. looked out for their own. She felt safe while working as long as she had Lexi with her.

Lexi stopped, lifted her head and barked

twice. She'd found the trail. "Good girl. Let's go."

Lexi ran hard, leading Valerie up the street. On the opposite side of the street, the dark car with the tinted windows remained. It was probably nothing. She had to let her unfounded fears go. She couldn't do her job if she was suspicious of everything.

Increasing her pace, Lexi pulled through to an alley that led into a residential neighborhood.

Valerie pushed the talk button on her shoulder mic. "I'm on State Street headed south pursuing suspects. I could use some backup."

"Captain McNeal is within a couple of blocks of your location," came the reply from dispatch.

It was unusual for her supervisor to be out on patrol at this hour. As captain of the Special Operations K-9 Unit, Slade McNeal had more than the lion's share of paperwork. Since his beloved K-9 partner, Rio, had been kidnapped by the syndicate, he had limited his time on patrol, utilizing Rio's father, Chief, when needed. A snitch with a long rap sheet had revealed to police that Rio was taken by the head of the local crime syndicate to find something in the Lost Woods, a huge forest on the outskirts of Sagebrush. The snitch was later found dead. The syndicate's structure was such that no one knew the identity of the leader, a man simply known as The Boss.

The loss of Rio over two months ago had been a blow to the whole department. These dogs weren't just useful resources—they were partners and beloved pets. Even though one of McNeal's well-to-do war buddies, Dante Frears, had offered a substantial reward of $25,000 for Rio's return, so far none of the leads had panned out.

Lexi pulled hard on the long canvas leash. Valerie couldn't trouble herself now with what McNeal was up to. After all, she had criminals to catch.

Lexi led Valerie through backyards and

over fences, past living rooms with illuminated television sets and houses with
dark windows. Though she saw no signs
of the suspects, Lexi's persistence told
her they were headed in the right direction. The scent trail that a person in flight
left was like a glow-in-the-dark line to a
dog's keen nose.

Lexi stopped suddenly in a yard that
had stacks of roofing shingles piled on the
walkway and a ladder propped against the
roof. Valerie had noticed another ladder
on the opposite side of the house, as well.
The dog circled and sniffed the ground
again. She'd lost the scent.

"What's going on, girl?"

In the distance, she heard the alto barking of a German shepherd. That had to
be McNeal with Chief. The insistence of
the barking suggested that Chief was onto
something.

Valerie talked to dispatch through her
shoulder mic. "Be advised. I am at 620
Kramer. Something is up with Lexi. The
trail may have gone cold."

Agitated, Lexi ran back and forth in the yard, stood by the ladder for a moment and then put her nose to the ground again. What was happening?

She watched Lexi pace the yard, running in all directions. The dog stopped, lifted her head and let out a single "Woof." She still had some kind of scent, but it was confusing her.

Chief's insistent barking reached her. He had definitely alerted to something. But what…? As the realization dawned on her, Valerie pushed her talk button. "I think our suspects split up."

"Copy that. We are sending another patrol unit your way. ETA is about five minutes."

The bushes in the yard across the fence shook. Valerie lifted her head just in time to see a man emerge. The look of fear and guilt on his face told her everything she needed to know.

"Stop! Sagebrush P.D."

The man took off running.

Lexi yanked on the leash, barking and

pulling wildly as the man ran around the back of the house. Knowing she couldn't crawl over the fence as fast as Lexi could jump it, Valerie clicked Lexi off the leash. The dog leapt over the fence and bounded after the suspect, her rapid-fire bark a clear sign that she was hot on the trail.

Her heart pumping, Valerie gripped her gun, prepared to run out to the sidewalk and through the gate to meet Lexi. She heard a scraping noise right before something crashed hard against her shoulder, knocking her to the ground.

Dazed by the impact, she stumbled to her feet. Shingles and a busted-open box spread across the walkway. She looked up. Was the second perpetrator on the roof? Had each of the three suspects run in a different direction?

Lexi's barking pressed hard on her ears, but grew farther away. The dog could handle herself. With her shoulder aching and still a little fuzzy headed, she hurried most of the way up the ladder using the roofline for cover.

She lifted her head up a few inches, catching movement by the chimney. "Sagebrush P.D. Drop your weapon." She ducked just as the whiz of a pistol shot shattered the night air. She fired off a round.

Silence.

She lifted her head a couple of inches. The suspect had come out from behind the chimney, aiming his gun at her.

He slipped on the sharply angled roof, falling on his side and dropping the gun. The gun skittered across the shingles and fell to the ground below. This was her chance. She didn't want him escaping down the ladder she'd seen on the other side of the house.

Valerie scrambled up the ladder, attempting to balance close to the top rung and aim her gun at the same time. "Put your hands up."

The man lifted his hands partway and then dropped them, dashing toward her. All the air left her lungs as fear enveloped her and she whispered a quick prayer. He intended to push the ladder away from the roof. She couldn't crawl down fast enough. She grabbed the ladder with her free hand as the man bolted toward her. It had been a stupid mistake to go up the ladder. She'd break her back if she fell that far.

The suspect's feet seemed to be pulled out from under him, and he was slammed facedown on the roof. Some unseen force pulled him backward away from her. As the suspect scrambled to his feet, she saw the silhouette of a second man, tall and broad through the shoulders.

The second man landed a blow to the suspect's face, knocking him on his back. The perp kicked the man's feet out from under him, and he slid down the steep angle of the roof toward the edge. He caught himself, pulling his body back up toward the suspect who sought refuge close to the chimney.

Valerie climbed onto the roof. Seeking to balance, she lifted her gun. "Put your hands up."

This time, the assailant complied. "I don't want to fall off here."

Neither did she. Valerie looked down and behind her. How on earth was she going to get this guy off here without killing herself and without giving him opportunity to run away?

The man who had helped her apprehend the perp stepped out of the shadows. "Officer Salgado, why don't you crawl down and wait at the bottom?" The man's hand went to a holster on his belt. "I'll stay up here and make sure this guy doesn't get any ideas."

She had no idea who this man was or where he had come from, but everything about him said law enforcement, and he knew her name. Still, this whole thing might have been a setup from the syndicate to get at her. "Who are you?" she shouted across the rooftop.

"FBI Agent Trevor Lewis. I rode in with Captain McNeal and saw that you were in trouble."

He sounded legit. She didn't have a lot

of choices and would have to check his I.D. later.

"Okay. I'll go down the ladder first," she said.

Agent Lewis held up his own gun. "I'll make sure this guy doesn't try to get off the roof by way of that other ladder."

She descended the ladder and waited while the suspect followed her. When his feet hit the ground, she pointed her gun at him. "Turn around, on the ground facedown, sir."

A look of hostility compressed his features, his lips curled. "I don't wanna go to jail. I'm innocent." The suspect stepped toward her with his hands out to grab her.

She adjusted her grip on the gun. "I said facedown on the ground, now."

"Do what the lady says," came the strong bass voice from the roof.

The perp tilted his head, grimaced and dropped to the ground.

Valerie pulled the cuffs from her belt. "You're innocent? Like everyone decides to shingle their roof at ten o'clock at night." She was still mad at herself for having climbed up the ladder. She'd broken a cardinal rule of training by putting herself in a vulnerable place.

Agent Lewis climbed to the bottom of the ladder. "At last, we meet." As Valerie stood up from cuffing the suspect, he held out his hand to her.

Why would an FBI agent want to greet her? Along the street, another black and white came to a stop, the additional backup dispatch had sent.

The screams of a man and a distant growl alerted Valerie to Lexi's progress with the other suspect. "Gotta go. Can you watch him until that officer over there can take him into custody?"

No time to wait around for Agent Trevor Lewis to explain why he was with McNeal. She raced out of the yard, pushing through the gate, following the sounds of the shrieking man. She wasn't worried about the suspect's safety; Lexi was trained to hold her suspect without biting. She just didn't want the man to claim police brutality because the dog had her teeth on the man for an excessive time.

She found the man in a grove of trees behind a house facedown with Lexi gripping his forearm in her teeth.

The man screamed in falsetto. "He's killing me. I don't want to die. Don't let that dog bite me."

"For your information, the dog is a she." Valerie clicked the dog into her leash. "Lex, off."

The dog complied but continued to lurch toward the suspect and bark. No one did their job with as much enthusiasm as Lexi. This dog loved to work.

A male officer came up behind Valerie. "That guy over there thought maybe you could use another set of handcuffs."

Valerie looked over at the man who had saved her life on the roof. Guess it was time to find out who Agent Trevor Lewis was and what he was doing showing up to help her on patrol.

* * *

Trevor watched the pretty redhead walk toward him. Maybe it was the green eyes bright in the evening lamplight, but there was something open and trusting in her expression as she drew close to him.

For the second time, he held out his hand. "Officer Salgado? Valerie Salgado?"

Still breathless from her pursuit, Valerie nodded and held out a hand. Her fingers were softer than silk, but her grip was strong and confident.

"Two suspects in custody, huh? Quite a night." Her decision to go up the ladder had seemed a little foolhardy, but she had handled herself well in every other way.

"I couldn't have done it without my partner." She kneeled, wrapping her arms about the thick-necked Rottweiler. "That's my girl." The dog's bobbed tail vibrated.

Valerie's shoulder mic made a glitchy noise. She pushed the receive button. "McNeal has the third suspect in custody. He's on his way over to talk to you as soon as he puts Chief back in the squad car."

"Copy. I'm standing on the six hundred block of Kramer Avenue. Agent Lewis is with me." Valerie commanded her dog to sit and turned toward Trevor. "So why did McNeal bring you out to meet me?"

Trevor stared down at the dog, who watched him with a wary eye. The dog was very protective of Valerie. "I just drove in from the San Antonio FBI office. I'm here to apprehend a fugitive…a Derek Murke."

Valerie shook her head. "The name's not ringing any bells for me."

The hope that this would be an easy capture faded. After two years of Murke popping up on the radar and then disappearing, why had he thought he could just breeze into town and Officer Salgado would know right where Murke was? "Captain McNeal thought you might have heard something. Murke spent his teen years here and has come back several times for extended stays. Since the fugitive used to live in some of the neighborhoods you patrol, the captain figured I could get your assistance in finding him."

"I'll help you as much as I can, but I can't neglect my regular patrol duties. What's he wanted for?"

"A few years ago, he robbed a bank in Phoenix." He'd spare her the longer version of the story, fearing he wouldn't be able to keep the emotion out of his voice.

Derek Murke wasn't just any fugitive. He was the fugitive who had shot rookie agent Cory Smith. Trevor had been Cory's training agent for his first field assignment. Cory Smith had been a little too eager to prove himself when he'd been a part of the apprehension team that had cornered Murke in a rental house. The kid hadn't waited for backup to be in place before entering the house. When Cory didn't assess his surroundings from all angles, Derek had seized the opportunity and shot him. Trevor would always wonder if he had given Cory too much responsibility too soon.

The sooner he had Murke in custody, the sooner he would feel like Cory's death hadn't been for nothing.

"I see introductions have already been made." He recognized Slade McNeal's voice behind him.

"Slade and I have done some joint drug task force work together," Trevor explained to Valerie.

McNeal placed his hands on his hips and looked at Valerie. "I thought maybe you could work with Agent Lewis to stir up some leads. He could tag along with you on your patrol, see if you can get any information for him. And in return, you get a little extra protection while you're on duty."

A shadow fell across Valerie's face. "I suppose I could use that."

McNeal excused himself to go talk to the officer hauling away one of the suspects.

Trevor watched him cross the street and then turned back to Valerie. "McNeal explained to me about the death threats

against you." News about the crime syndicate Sagebrush was battling had reached
other parts of the state. Now as he watched
the tall redhead's demeanor change from
confident to fearful, all the news stories
and police reports seemed a lot more personal. "I'm glad to help out."

The black and white disappeared around
the corner. McNeal walked back toward
them.

"I'm on the morning shift tomorrow."
She still seemed guarded. "I assume you
have some sort of file on this guy Murke?
Maybe there is something in there that
will give me an idea of where to look for
him."

She wasn't exactly warming to the idea
of an FBI agent tagging along. "I won't
waste your on-duty time if I don't have to.
I can bring it by before you go on shift. If
nothing in the file helps, maybe McNeal
has some other ideas."

"That would be fine." Valerie wrote
down her home address. As she was
handing him the card, her gaze shifted

from his face to over his shoulder. Her eyes grew wide as a look of apprehension clouded her features.

Trevor turned, following the line of her gaze. Across the street, a black car with tinted windows slowed to a crawl before speeding up and disappearing around a corner. Alerting on something, Lexi rose from her haunches.

He turned back toward Valerie. Her lips were drawn into a hard, straight line. Something about that black car had upset her.

"Is everything okay?"

She took a step back, shaking her head. "It's…it's nothing." She squared her shoulders and lifted her chin, but her effort at bravado fell short. He could see the fear in her eyes.

Valerie Salgado was living with a death threat hanging over her head. Maybe the car had just slowed down to look for an address, but it had bothered her. Anger flooded through him over the syndicate's stronghold on her life.

If they did end up working together, she wasn't going to die on his watch.

TWO

Valerie peered out the front window of her house. In the early-morning light, she could make out the outline of the police car parked outside. She drew her eighteen-month-old niece, Bethany, closer.

Would she ever get used to that sight? Would there ever be a time when her life wasn't shrouded in danger?

Knowing that the car with the dark windows had been following her last night drove the point home. The syndicate wasn't going to go away. They were just waiting for the right moment to get at her. Sagebrush police knew that one of the middle managers was a woman. That woman, whose street name was Serpent, was most likely the woman Valerie had seen. The Serpent had no way of knowing Valerie couldn't identify her yet. She probably thought it was just a matter of time before she was picked up.

A chill skittered over Valerie's skin when she thought of the woman's eyes meeting hers on the street. Seemingly yellow in the lamplight, they bore right through Valerie. The memory still invaded her thoughts and sent a current of fear through her.

Bethany shifted in Valerie's arms. She jerked her head back and blinked several times. She was all blue eyes and soft downy hair, just like her mother. Kathleen's funeral had been more than a month ago, but it still felt so raw. While the cancer had slowly drained the vitality out of Valerie's older sister, it had given her time to express that she wanted Valerie to take care of Bethany. The child's father had never been in the picture and had signed away rights even before Bethany was born. Though she felt ill equipped for the job, Valerie intended to keep her promise to her beloved sister.

Valerie held Bethany close, absorbing her softness and that sweet baby smell. Over the months, Valerie had slowly been taking over mothering duties as Kathleen grew weaker. But since Kathleen's death, Bethany had not slept through the night. Though the little girl couldn't articulate it, Valerie knew she was mourning.

Even now, Bethany clung to the stuffed pink rabbit Kathleen had given her. She hardly ever let go of the toy. Valerie swayed back and forth. "I know, you miss your mama." A lump formed in her throat. "I miss her, too."

Bethany melted against Valerie. After a few minutes, the little girl relaxed and her breathing steadied, asleep at last. Valerie padded on stocking feet toward the stairs that led to the bedroom, careful not to jostle the sleeping baby. She glanced at the living room clock.

She stopped so suddenly that Bethany wiggled in her arms. Where had the time gone? She should have been ready for work by now. The sitter would be here any minute. It was easy enough to lose track of time when you got up four or five times in the night to deal with a fussy toddler.

A knock came at her door, loud and intense. Lexi sauntered out of her crate positioned by the sliding glass door. She raised her head and looked toward Valerie, expecting instructions.

Valerie turned toward the door. "Who is it?"

"Trevor Lewis."

And she was still in her bathrobe. What had she been thinking when she had agreed to him swinging by before work? Now that she had Bethany, it took her twice as long to get ready in the morning. Valerie gave the Rottweiler a reassuring look. "Go back to sleep, Lexi. It's okay."

"Just a second." After placing Bethany in her playpen, Valerie took a breath to calm her nerves. She hoped she hadn't seemed too standoffish to Agent Lewis last night. McNeal had been looking out for her when he suggested she work with Trevor, and maybe she'd be able to help him. She probably needed the extra protection, but the partnership was a bitter reminder of how hard the syndicate was making it for her to do her job.

She swung open the door. Trevor looked fresh in a crisp, French blue button-down shirt. His dark curly hair was clipped close to his head and his brown eyes had an intensity she hadn't noticed last night.

His gaze fell to her bathrobe, and heat rushed up her face. "My little one has me running behind schedule." She turned slightly away from the door so Trevor had a view of Bethany shaking the sides of her playpen.

Barely acknowledging the child, Trevor lifted the computer tablet he had in his hand. "I've got Murke's file."

"Come in. I need just a minute to get ready," she said.

Trevor glanced around the room. "Where's the dog?"

"She's resting in her crate." Valerie sighed as she looked at the crate and then at the playpen not too far from it. Lexi had never shown any aggression toward Bethany, but the dog was keeping her distance. Though Lexi was protective of Valerie, it would be a shame if she didn't bond with Bethany. The trainer at the K-9 facility had assured her that dogs were just like people—it took time for them to adjust to new situations.

"Take a seat, Mr. Lewis."

"You can call me Trevor."

Bethany babbled and held her hands up. Valerie gathered her into her arms and grabbed her bottle off the counter. When Valerie offered it to her, Bethany shook her head. She hadn't eaten anything yet this morning. Valerie tried not to give in to worry. She bounced Bethany in her arms. "We don't want you losing weight."

She had fifteen minutes before her neighbor, Stella Witherspoon, came over to watch Bethany. Not enough time to get everything done. This motherhood thing was a juggling act and so far she had dropped all her balls.

She sat Bethany on the opposite side of the couch from Trevor. Valerie smoothed Bethany's silky, soft hair and then handed Trevor the bottle. "If Bethany starts to fuss, see if she will take this."

Trevor's eyes grew wide with fear. "Give her the bottle?" His voice slipped up half an octave.

Valerie shook her head. "It would be a help." You'd think she had asked him to split an atom.

Still flustered by all she had to get done in a short amount of time, Valerie went up the stairs to where her uniform was laid out.

Trevor Lewis shifted uneasily on the couch. The little girl stuck two fingers in her mouth and watched him. With her free hand, she held on to a stuffed pink bunny that had seen better days. One of its ears dangled by a thread. He didn't know that much about kids, but she looked at him like he was a pinned insect.

"Is your name Bethany?"

She continued to stare and suck her fingers. Did kids this little talk?

Valerie seemed distracted. Did she even want to work with him? He stared down at the tablet where he had opened Derek Murke's file. Trying to catch a fugitive without the cooperation of the local police department never went well. She was the most likely candidate to help him. McNeal had mentioned that Salgado was a rookie…just like Cory Smith had been. Icy pain stabbed at Trevor's heart. Could he keep this rookie safe?

Trevor let out a heavy breath and looked at Bethany. And she had a kid.

He held up the bottle to Bethany. "You want this?"

Bethany popped her fingers out of her mouth. She pointed at something across the room and said, "Gaga."

He had no idea what she was talking about. Being around babies made him feel awkward. They seemed so fragile. As if they would shatter like glass if you didn't hold them right. Bethany flipped around to her belly and slid off the couch. She tottered over to him, blue eyes still assessing him.

Her hand rested on his leg with a touch that was barely heavier than air. He held the bottle toward her while she was still standing and fed her as though she were a newborn lamb. She looked up at him with eyes that were filled with trust. He felt a fluttering in his heart. How unexpected that this delicate child was okay with him feeding her.

When he glanced around the room, Valerie stood at the base of the stairs watching them. Without the utility belt, the uniform accentuated her curves. Her red hair had been pulled up into a ponytail, revealing the soft lines of her face and clear green eyes.

"You can hold her, you know." There was a hint of amusement in her voice.

"We're doing just fine," Trevor muttered.

Bethany pulled away from him and tottered toward Valerie just as the doorbell rang. An older woman with white, fluffy hair that had a tint of blue to it stepped across the threshold when Valerie opened the door. Valerie introduced the babysitter as Stella Witherspoon.

"There's my little Bethie." Mrs. Witherspoon's voice had a charming bell-like quality.

The little girl squealed with delight and kicked her legs while Valerie held her. "Thanks for coming, Stella."

Bethany nestled against Valerie while she gave Stella instructions for the day. Valerie ran a finger down Bethany's cheek and rubbed noses with her when the little girl tilted her head up. She seemed like a natural at being a mom. Where was the baby's father in all this? He hadn't noticed a wedding band on her finger.

After Valerie handed Bethany over, she turned toward Trevor. "Since I'm running late, I can look at the file on the way to the station." She turned back toward the kitchen. "Lexi, come."

The dog trotted out from her crate by the back door.

Valerie grabbed the leash and canine vest by the door and proceeded to put them on Lexi. She rose to her feet. "I hope you don't mind. She goes everywhere with me while I'm on duty."

Trevor nodded. "I understand." He opened the door for her when she had clicked Lexi into her leash.

As they stepped out into the early morning, light shimmered across Valerie's coppery hair. She stopped and stared at where the police car used to be.

"I sent him home since you're with me," Trevor said.

Her voice took on that soft, distant quality. "He usually follows me into the station in the morning."

The inflection in her voice suggested weariness, as though the need for protection had taken its toll on her emotionally.

Trevor glanced around. Other than automated sprinklers turning on, he saw no movement anywhere on the quiet street. He sidled closer to Valerie.

She turned toward him, furling her brow. "You don't need to stand quite so close. I'm a trained officer. I can handle myself."

He had to remind himself that though her irritation was directed toward him, she was probably more upset about the loss of freedom the death threats had created. "I don't doubt you can handle yourself."

She opened the back door of Trevor's sedan to let Lexi in.

On the drive toward the station, Trevor filled Valerie in on the investigation as she flipped through the file. "We knew that Sagebrush was one of the places Murke had ties to. He lived here during his teen years and has come back several times since. He's on the FBI's Most Wanted list, so his picture has been out there. We had an anonymous tip, someone who saw him in a store here in Sage-brush."

Valerie stared at the photo of Murke on the tablet. "Sometimes people are mistaken about identities." She flicked through the pages of the file.

"I know that. It makes sense, though, that Murke would come back here," he said as doubt tapped at the corners of his awareness. Valerie had to find something that would give them a lead. The urgency to catch Murke was stronger than ever.

Valerie looked up from the tablet. Her eyes lit up as they passed a schoolyard just starting to fill with children. She really seemed to gravitate toward kids. Having kids, being married, none of that had ever been on his radar. His father had been a brute of a man, cruel beyond reason. If it hadn't been for a youth pastor, who had turned his heart toward God, Trevor could have gone down that same road. The way he had it figured, he didn't want to risk having those patterns of violence emerge in his own life. He was a better help to humanity as a lawman.

"So it's just you and Bethany?" The question had spilled out. He had to admit, he was curious.

Valerie laced her fingers together and bent her head. "Bethany is my sister's child. I recently became her guardian when Kathleen died." Her voice trembled.

Trevor retreated, aware that he had stepped on an emotional land mine. "Well, you seem like a natural mom."

Her face glowed, and her voice fused with warmth. "Thanks. It's been an adjustment for both of us."

He hadn't counted on the compliment meaning so much to her. He took a quick sideways glance at her. Shorter hair that had escaped the ponytail framed her soft features, and her full mouth curled into a faint smile. Was she still thinking about what he had said?

Valerie looked back down at the tablet. "Murke robbed a pawn shop with a guy named Leroy Seville?"

Trevor's spirits lifted. "Yeah, do you know him?"

"No, but I know an elderly lady named Linda Seville. I don't think she ever said anything about a son, but they could be related."

"It's worth a shot." This could be the lead he had hoped for.

She lifted her head and peered through the windshield. "We're actually pretty close to where she lives. Let's just go there now. Four blocks up and one over." She paused. "I know the street, and I'll remember the house when I see it."

He caught a whiff of her floral perfume as she leaned closer to him to point through the windshield. He leaned toward her as his stomach tightened.

He pulled to the curb, scanning the area as he got out of the car. "This is the street?" The neighborhood consisted of older homes built close together and several apartment buildings.

She looked at him over the top of the car. "Yep, this is the neighborhood I patrol." She spoke with affection as she lifted her chin and looked around. "If I remember correctly, I met Linda on a stolen television case." She studied the line of houses as though she was trying to jar her memory about where Linda Seville lived.

A girl of about seven road by on a bike. "Hey, Officer Salgado."

A trilling laugh escaped Valerie's throat. "Hey, Jessie Lynn. I see you found a new chain for your bike."

The kid was half a block away when she shouted, "Yes, ma'am, I did."

She turned to face Trevor. "Jessie loves that bike. She always gets a ride in before school."

Valerie cared about the people here. That much was clear, but sometimes emotions got in the way of the job. He hoped she could keep them in check.

Valerie came around the car and joined Trevor on the sidewalk. She looked up at him, expectation coloring her lovely features. She had a spray of freckles across her nose and cheeks, and her voice had a soft quality that made him think of lullabies. He shook himself free of the warm, fuzzy feeling he got when she stood close to him. Okay, she was attractive and smelled nice. So what? He had a job to do.

Valerie pointed to a bungalow-style house with flower beds that were overgrown with weeds. "That's it, right there. Now I remember. It wasn't a stolen television—it was a missing pet."

It sounded like Valerie didn't know Linda Seville all that well. They made their way up the sidewalk. Worry twisted into a hard knot at the base of his stomach. What if this lead didn't pan out? Would they be back to square one?

As though she had read his mind, Valerie said, "We might be able to get a line on Murke some other way if this turns out to be nothing."

He appreciated her optimism, but in his mind, there were no second shots. Murke had evaded him since Cory's death, leaving whatever town he'd drifted into the second he got wind that the Bureau was onto him. The capture needed to be swift before Murke had a chance to run again.

He knocked on the door. Through the sheer curtain, he could see that all the lights had been turned off, and no one stirred inside. He could feel that tightening in his chest. That awful feeling that they'd missed their chance to get the jump on Murke. "Where would this Linda be if she wasn't at home?" He couldn't hide the urgency in his voice.

"I don't know that much about her. She's not one of the people in the neighborhood who talks to me. I just helped her find her poodle months ago." She turned and looked at the other houses. "I'm sure we can ask around."

Trevor tensed. Too much asking around meant a greater chance of Murke getting wind that the Bureau had found him. "I just want this lead to work out."

She flinched as though he had hit her with his words. "You really want to get this guy, don't you?"

Trevor softened his tone. She didn't deserve to be the recipient of the frustration over his long history with Murke. "He shot an agent I was training. Cory was a rookie fresh out of the Academy, and I know rookies make rookie mistakes, but he didn't deserve to die."

"I'm sorry about the agent being shot." An emotion flashed across her face that almost looked like hurt, though he couldn't figure out why. "I don't think she's here." Valerie turned away and stared up the street.

He'd heard the quiver in her voice. Something he had said had struck a nerve. Women made him crazy sometimes. He was always saying the wrong thing around them and never quite understanding why it had been the wrong thing. Trying to sort it out with her would just make things worse.

Just let it go and do your job.

Trevor scanned the windows of the apartment buildings. No doubt the neighborhood had eyes everywhere. They'd expect to see Officer Salgado around, but would wonder what he was doing here. And then they would start to talk. If Murke was in this neighborhood, how long before word got back to him?

When he turned toward Valerie, she still had her back to him. She let out a soft gasp as her shoulders stiffened and she reached for her gun. He followed the line of her gaze.

Derek Murke sidled up the street holding two plastic bags and a six-pack of beer.

THREE

"Police, stop."

Valerie sprinted across the grass and drew her weapon.

Shock registered on Murke's face. He dropped his groceries and dashed up the alley.

Murke was headed for the warehouses behind the bungalows. Valerie called out to Trevor. "Stay with him. I'll grab Lexi."

Trevor had already drawn his handgun. He raced past her down the alley. Murke bolted over a dilapidated fence with Trevor on his heels.

Valerie ran to Trevor's car and opened the back door for Lexi. With the dog pulling hard on the leash, Valerie circled around the fence. She entered a two-block area containing a series of metal buildings, some still in use and others abandoned. She saw no sign of Murke or Trevor. She took Lexi over to the other side of the fence where Murke had probably landed. Lexi picked up the trail right away.

They jogged past a tire shop that was still operational, but closed at this hour. There was a risk that Lexi had picked up on Trevor's scent and not Murke's since both men were running. Following a scent was not a perfect science, but she'd trust Lexi's nose over searching blindly.

Heart pounding, she took in her surroundings as she ran. The Rottweiler pulled toward a large warehouse. Metal slapped against metal. The sound of a door slamming against the frame or the wind blowing? Valerie followed Lexi into the warehouse through a place in the exterior wall where the corrugated metal had been bent back from the frame.

Once inside, she waited for her eyes to adjust to the dimness. The warehouse was a big open area with a balcony all around it. This had been a clothing factory at one time. Pieces of abandoned equipment provided numerous places for Murke to hide. Trevor might have lost sight of him and gone off in the wrong direction.

She studied the stairs leading up to the balcony where the offices used to be. Now they were just gaping holes, the office doors having long since been looted.

Lexi kept her nose to the ground, though her pace slowed.

A creak of floorboards caused Valerie to turn. She waited for another sign of life. If Murke was close, Lexi would have been more excited. Valerie licked her dry lips. Blood whooshed in her ears as she adjusted her grip on the gun. Water dripped somewhere in the building. The steady tap, tap, tap of the droplets hitting metal overtook the leaden silence.

Lexi ran back and forth. The scent had become muddled.

Though Valerie's hands remained steady, sweat trickled down her back. Someone was in here. She could feel eyes watching her. Lexi stopped sniffing and lifted her head.

Valerie tuned in to the sounds around her as she breathed in the musty air. Lexi's panting became more pronounced.

Seconds passed. The sense that she was being watched had been with her since the Andrew Garry murder. Was she just imagining it now? She'd give anything to replay the tape of her life and go back to that night—to make different choices. When she'd passed that woman wearing the hooded jacket on the street, something had seemed amiss…but she had ignored her instincts. The next day, Garry's body had been found by another K-9 unit. By then, the woman had disappeared.

Valerie's father, a retired detective, had always said that instinct was a cop's best asset. She had made a stupid rookie mistake and ignored the prickling of the hairs on her neck when that woman had looked at her. Trevor Lewis had no idea that his comment about rookies making mistakes was like a dagger through her chest.

Her life would have been different if she had followed her gut and stopped to engage the woman in conversation. The woman's guilt might have risen to the surface, and Valerie could have detained her for questioning. She certainly would have gotten a better look at the person who later became their prime suspect.

Another noise jerked Valerie away from her regret and back into the warehouse. The balcony creaked. Was the wind blowing through here strong enough to do that? She examined the balcony segment by segment.

Lexi sniffed the ground and then sneezed.

"He got away." A voice boomed in her ear.

Though her training kept her from dropping the gun, the voice had startled her. "Agent Lewis, do you always creep up on people like that?"

"Sorry, you were so focused on that balcony, there was no way not to surprise you." The arch of his eyebrow and slight upturn of his mouth suggested amusement.

Valerie holstered her gun and squared her shoulders, hoping he hadn't picked up on her loss of composure. She should have heard him coming no matter how closely she was watching the balcony. Tunnel vision while on duty could be deadly. Another stupid rookie mistake. She steadied her voice. "Murke got away?" She pointed to the dog who was working her way to the opposite side of the warehouse. "Lexi picked up on something in here."

"The dog's right. He did run through here, but then he doubled back and went out to the street."

That explained why the scent had become muddled for Lexi.

"I caught up with him on the street." Frustration was evident in Trevor's voice. "He got into a car and took off. No way could I catch him. But I know the make and model, and the first two letters on the plate. We'll post notices out to the locals and the highway patrol. Murke will most likely try to leave town now that he knows we're on to him."

She surveyed the warehouse one more time. She had to let go of the idea that the syndicate could be everywhere and was watching her. "Guess we better get back to the station."

She couldn't read Trevor's expression, but his voice softened. "Maybe next time we need to work on not getting separated like that," he said.

His tone of concern touched her, but she needed to be able to do her job. "Splitting up is standard procedure. Lexi can be a real asset in these situations."

"Sometimes there are things that are more important than procedure," he said.

The smolder in his voice made her heart flutter. Was he that worried about her well-being? He barely knew her.

He stepped closer to her, his hand brushing her forearm. "I said I'd protect you. I don't want to break my promise to McNeal."

Was that all it was about, keeping his word to an old buddy? She struggled to let go of her disappointment. And then wondered why it had even mattered to her that he had expressed concern for her that seemed to go beyond work requirements. "I have paperwork to catch up on back at the station. I still have to do my regular job." She headed toward the door of the warehouse, yanking on Lexi's leash. The dog was reluctant to leave the spot where she'd picked up the scent again. "Come on, Lex."

Once they were in his car, Valerie directed Trevor to the Sagebrush Police Station, a one-story, red-brick building. She led him around to the back where the K-9 officers had a separate entrance. She could feel his body heat and sense his proximity as he walked behind her. There was no chance of them being separated now.

He was one of those men who seemed to live in a state of heightened alert anyway, and he was taking watching her back seriously. Asking him to hang back a little ways wouldn't do any good. She'd just have to get used to it for the time being. "I've got some reports to complete, and I'll pull Leroy Seville's file to see if I can find out anything more. I'm sure I'll be safe at my desk."

Trevor took a step back. "Great...I'll brief the other officers in the station on Murke. Then maybe we can see if we can track down this Linda Seville lady, find out if Murke was staying at her house or just somewhere on that street." His voice became more intense. "We need to jump on this. Murke is famous for leaving town as soon as he knows we're closing in on him."

As she and Lexi passed the other K-9 officers' desks, a black lab lay by Detective Jackson Worth's chair while he bent over a report. Titan lifted his head when she passed by but didn't move. The lab's job was to stick near Jackson, to watch over him. The devotion of the dogs to their handlers filled her with gratitude.

Truth was, she felt safe as long as Lexi stayed close. The dogs remained with the officers most of the time, because having the K-9 as a pet as well as a partner was the best way to ensure unwavering obedience.

Valerie scooted her chair up to her desk and opened up a database that listed Sagebrush felons. Leroy Seville was recently out on parole after five years in jail. Linda Seville was listed as an emergency contact and identified as his great-aunt. They could catch up with Leroy later and see what he knew about Murke. She doubted Murke would go back to Linda's home.

In the small Sagebrush station, Trevor's warm bass voice carried across the room as he showed Murke's picture to the other officers. She tried to focus on her computer screen instead of the joking that seemed to be going on between Trevor and the other officers.

She adjusted her chair for the umpteenth time and leaned closer to the monitor. Trevor hadn't hidden his ire at getting close to Murke, yet not catching him. Did he blame her for that? It was her own insecurity that made her wonder if he was fishing around for a different officer to assist him.

She could only pick up bits and pieces of the conversation, and yet she had assumed that that was what was going on. Why did she even care? Having to help Trevor took away time from her regular work.

Okay, so he didn't like rookies. McNeal had paired them up for a reason. It couldn't just be because it was extra protection for her. Trevor wasn't going to ditch her for a more experienced officer who didn't have any connection to the neighborhoods where Murke was likely to be. Valerie chided herself for worrying. Fine with her if he wanted to work with a different officer.

She picked up a pen, making lines on a legal pad so deep they nearly cut through the paper. That caring tone he had used back at the warehouse had messed with her initial impression of him—that he was one of those lawmen who was good at his job but not so good at connecting with people. Maybe there was some chink in his armor. It wasn't her job to try to find it. The sooner they caught Murke, the sooner Trevor Lewis would be gone.

Pushing all thoughts of the impossibly handsome agent out of her head, she focused on the monitor, opening up a report she needed to complete. The voices around her faded, and all she heard was the tapping of the keys....

She completed the report and opened her email. She smiled as she read the thank-you notes from children at a school where she and Lexi had given a K-9 demonstration. She loved teaching members of the community about what the K-9 units did.

An email from her mother caught her attention as she scrolled down. Her mother usually used her private email. Her skin prickled as apprehension invaded her body.

She opened it up and read.

Bethany is such a pretty baby. It would be a shame to have anything happen to her.

The temperature in the room seemed to drop ten degrees as she stared at the computer screen. It was clear what had happened. Her mother would never send such a horrible email. So now the syndicate was hacking into family members' emails and threatening the life of her niece?

Her hands were shaking as she grabbed the phone to dial her home number.

Stella picked up on the first ring. "Hello."

Valerie took a breath, hoping to hide the anxiety in her voice. "Hey, Mrs. Witherspoon, I was just checking to see how Bethany was doing."

Stella's voice exuded cheerfulness. "She's such a doll. She just finished her cereal and is playing with her blocks."

"So, everything's okay?"

"Couldn't be better." Stella paused as though she were thinking something over. "Are you having a little separation anxiety, dear?"

Valerie gripped the phone a little tighter. "That must be it."

"It happens to every mother. Call here a thousand times a day if you need to."

Though she couldn't let go of the fear over harm coming to Bethany, Valerie relaxed a little. Bethany was in good hands. "Mrs. Witherspoon, you are an answer to prayer."

Valerie said her goodbyes and hung up. She called her mother who said she didn't think her email had been hacked. She barely turned her computer on. These guys were good. She pressed her trembling hands, palms down against the desk. Tuned into Valerie's heightened emotion, Lexi lifted her head and looked at her with dark brown eyes.

The words echoed through her mind. *It would be a shame if anything happened to her.* She felt like she was being shaken from the inside. Would Garry's murderer hurt Bethany to get to her? Now she knew for sure she was being watched. They must have seen her with Bethany.

"Everything okay?" Trevor stood beside her desk.

She straightened her spine and squared her shoulders, forcing her voice to sound professional. "Sure. Why?"

He sat down in the chair beside her, concern etched across his face. "Your complexion's the color of rice."

"It's nothing." She couldn't explain to him. He wouldn't understand why she was so upset. It was just an email, right? It wasn't like a gun had been pointed at her. "My face is always this color. I'm a light-skinned redhead."

He cracked a smile. "That you are, Officer Salgado, but that doesn't explain why your hands are shaking." He reached over and cupped his hand over hers.

She'd laced her fingers together so tightly her knuckles were white. He pulled back and studied her while the warmth of his touch lingered. Would he think she lacked strength as an officer if she revealed how much the threat had shaken her up? Cops were supposed to have titanium spines, right? There probably wasn't anything in the world that made Trevor Lewis afraid…except maybe feeding babies.

The warmth in his eyes, the same that she had seen at the warehouse, told her she could risk sharing.

She drew in a breath and turned the computer monitor toward him. "I just got this." She pulled the photo of Bethany off her cubicle wall and held it to her chest. Images about bad things happening to Bethany rampaged through her head. She shivered.

Trevor's jaw hardened as he looked away from the screen. He shook his head. "Unbelievable. This has got to be the syndicate's doing. Your mother would never send an email like that, right?"

Valerie nodded. "Who else would do this but the syndicate? The first threat came in an email, as well."

His presence had a calming effect on her that she didn't understand. Maybe it was just because he looked like he could smash small buildings with his fist. Being able to share with him had eased her fear. Now that she could get a deep breath, she felt like she was seeing things more clearly. "They wouldn't actually hurt Bethany, would they? It's me the Serpent is after."

"It doesn't matter if they will or won't. They are threatening your kid and upsetting you. It's all part of a game they're playing." His tone suggested deep offense at what had been done to her.

She exhaled. "It might be that it was meant to scare me. You know, the syndicate's reminder that they are still watching and waiting for their chance to kill me." She just didn't want to believe that anyone would harm an innocent child.

Trevor touched his clean-shaven face as his eyes narrowed. "I've seen this before with witnesses we were trying to protect. The intent is to break you psychologically. You don't want something bad to happen to your kid, so you back off from finding this woman."

"I can't even identify the woman yet for sure. We haven't been able to put together a sketch or a police lineup." She turned back to her computer and clicked out of her email program. "I just know that if I saw this woman that we think is the Serpent again, I would recognize her."

Trevor sat back in his chair. "The murderer doesn't know that, though. She probably thinks it's just a matter of time before the Sagebrush police track her down. These people are ruthless. They'll do everything they can to shake your resolve."

"I wish there was protection for Bethany when I'm not with her." Talking with Trevor had eased some of her fear, but every time she looked at Bethany's picture, she felt a jab to her heart. If anything happened to that little girl....

"Maybe the department can provide some protection," Trevor suggested.

"I can ask, and I'll let the captain know about the email, but it's always a funding and resources issue," she said.

At the other end of the administrative area, Captain McNeal stepped out of his office. "Dispatch just got a call from a black and white downtown. The car you saw Murke drive away in has been spotted outside a hardware store on Sagebrush Boulevard."

Valerie jumped up and grabbed Lexi's leash. "We might have Murke in custody before the day is over." Excitement pulsed through her. Chasing down Murke would get her mind off the email.

She clicked Lexi into her leash, glad to be doing something she could deal with.

Trevor quickened his pace as he moved toward the door. "Let's go catch a fugitive."

FOUR

Adrenaline surged through Valerie as Trevor selected a parking space with a view of Derek Murke's older-model Buick parked across the street. Murke was nowhere in sight. He had to be in one of the shops. She loved this part of the job—the prospect of catching a criminal brought the importance of her work back to her.

The sidewalks bustled with afternoon activity. Downtown Sagebrush was a mixture of boutiques and restaurants that provided a medley of rustic charm and trendy affluency. She recognized the patrol car up the block and two other unmarked police cars that had moved into place. Now it was just a matter of sitting and waiting. Murke had to come back to his car sooner or later.

Lexi leaned forward and panted.

Trevor angled his head away so he wouldn't get slobbered on.

"Sorry, she just likes to be a part of the action," Valerie explained, smiling indulgently as she stroked Lexi's ears.

The radio sparked to life. "Car two this is car one. I've got eyes on Murke. He's standing at the check-out line in Bealman's Hardware."

Trevor lurched in his seat. "All right, let's move in. Keep the uniforms out of sight range. I don't want Murke to know we're on to him."

Valerie sat back in her seat trying to hide her disappointment. "I guess that means me, too." She looked down at her uniform.

"He scares easily." He'd already pushed open the door and slipped out of the car. "Radio the other units of his position if you see him."

Trevor attempted a casual but hurried walk across the street. Two other plain-clothes officers were making a beeline for the hardware store. Valerie scanned the surrounding shops and the street. Though she accepted the reason for the decision, she really didn't like being put out of commission like this.

If Murke did come this way, her response time would be faster if she and Lexi were already on the street. If he was on the run already, it wouldn't matter if he saw her uniform.

She slipped out of the car, removed Lexi from the backseat and walked up the boulevard, keeping her eyes on the exterior of the hardware store. She shielded herself behind the other pedestrians to avoid being spotted. She walked past Arianna's Diner and a boutique that sold hats and other accessories.

A voice came across her shoulder mic. "Stand down. False alarm. Bad I.D."

Across the street, Trevor emerged from a cluster of people on the sidewalk. The droop in his shoulders communicated his level of disappointment as he made his way to the end of the block. Valerie's awareness switched into high gear. She turned in a half circle. Murke was still skulking around here. He hadn't come back to his car parked close to the hardware store. Sooner or later, he would show.

Walking to the end of the block, she kept her eye on Murke's car. Parking was at a premium in the downtown area. Just because he had parked by the hardware store didn't mean that was where he went. Trevor was doing the same sort of walking surveillance on the other side of the street. One of them needed to get back to the car in case they ended up tailing Murke in a vehicle. She turned and headed back toward the car.

Lexi came to attention and peered up the street. Valerie shifted her gaze. Murke had just stepped out of Arianna's Diner holding two take-out boxes. Recognition spread across his face as he narrowed his dark soulless eyes at her.

She expected Murke to turn and bolt… to make a beeline for his car. Instead, as she drew within feet of him, he charged toward her. Soda and a take-out box filled with a pasta dish showered down on her and Lexi. The crowd around them scattered like cockroaches in the light.

In the few seconds it took her to recover, Murke pivoted and raced up the street. He disappeared into a cluster of people. Murke's dirty-blond head bobbed up right before he entered a men's clothing store. She dashed inside.

Lexi sneezed repeatedly from the spices that had gone up her nose. The dog couldn't focus on Murke's scent trail. Valerie squinted as her eyes adjusted to the dim lighting. Behind the counter, a clerk pointed toward the back door. Valerie hurried into the alley. The sounds of the busy street gave way to a quiet alley. She heard footsteps and ran in the direction of them.

The alley smelled of garbage and Mexican spices and chemicals from a dry cleaners. A door creaked open, and a man came out tossing a trash bag in an open Dumpster. He offered Valerie only a passing glance before going back inside as if cops with K-9 units chased fugitives up this alley every day.

Trevor's comment about them staying together came back to her, but she swiped the thought from her mind. Doing her job had to be priority one. She needed to catch this guy. He'd already killed one lawman.

She radioed her location. Trevor and the others had to have seen the disruption on the street. They were probably already running this way.

Lexi dutifully placed her nose on the ground and sniffed. Then she sneezed. Would Lexi be able to pick up the scent?

She heard no further noise. Unless he'd slipped into the back door of one of the shops, Murke had to be hiding somewhere. She searched each nook and cranny, opened Dumpsters and checked behind a pile of crates.

Lexi pulled a little harder on her leash. "You got something, girl?"

The dog ran toward a stairway that led

to a second-floor door. Valerie remained down below with her gun drawn prepared to shoot if Murke was behind the door.

A voice as cold as ice sounded in her ear as the hard blade of a knife pressed against her throat. "Drop the gun."

Her heart lurched. She let the gun fall to the ground.

Lexi was already headed back down the stairs. Murke hadn't noticed the dog.

Hurry girl, hurry.

Valerie let her hands go limp as though she would comply. When she felt his body relax, she slammed her elbow hard into his stomach. Murke groaned. She turned to face her attacker, preparing to land a second blow.

She saw his face, features compressed into an expression of hate. Onyx eyes tore through her. Behind her, Lexi barked.

Murke's eyes grew wide with fear when he saw Lexi. He took off running again. Lexi bolted past her hot on Murke's heels but was slowed down by her sneezing. It took only a moment for Valerie to retrieve her gun and chase after Murke.

Trevor raced through a store that sold Western wear, past puzzled clerks and out the back entrance. A mixture of fear and anger warred inside him. He had told Valerie to stay in the car. Why hadn't she listened? The uniform thing had been his excuse to keep her safe.

It had taken less than three minutes to figure out it was Valerie and Murke causing the ruckus across the street. Her red hair had flashed bright in the noonday sun, then he had darted across the street to find her.

He stepped out of the Western shop into the empty alley. Where had she gone? His heart squeezed tight. All anger washed away as fear took over. What if Murke had killed her?

Not again. God, please, not again.

He scanned up and down the alley, pushing down the rising panic. She had to be all right.

The distant bark of the dog brought a sense of relief. That had to be Lexi. He followed the sound of the barking, heading away from downtown and toward a residential part of Sagebrush. His feet pounded on the sidewalk as he ran past yards just starting to turn green. He stopped to listen again for the barking. He caught up with Valerie and Lexi by some playground equipment that was part of a housing complex.

She turned to face him as he approached. "We lost sight of him." She looked down at Lexi, who sat at her feet, panting. "Her sniffer is all messed up. Daytime searches are harder anyway—too many people running around, lot of scents to sort through."

"One of the units is still watching the car. If he tries to go back that way, we'll nab him." Disappointment settled in his stomach like a rock. Twice in one day, Murke had been within his grasp...and he had eluded them.

"I already radioed a patrol unit to comb the streets." She tugged on Lexi's leash.

"We'll walk the neighborhood, see if we can pick up on anything. Maybe somebody saw him."

Trevor stood close to Valerie, expecting to be enveloped in her floral scent. Instead, he smelled...Italian spices? Her uniform had stains on it. "What happened to you?"

"Murke's escape plan involved throwing his takeout at me. Lexi got spices up her nose, and Murke's lunch is all over my uniform." She shook her head and rolled her eyes. "Let's not make a big deal about it or else the other officers will have a nickname for me before the day is over."

"I don't know...you might have started a trend. Marinara-scented perfume could become very popular," he quipped.

She had an easy laugh that helped quell some of the frustration he'd felt at losing Murke again.

They searched the street for several more hours before giving up. The Buick remained parked by the hardware store. Murke wouldn't be stupid enough to return. Maybe he had slipped into a garage or an unlocked house and maybe he had phoned someone and gotten a ride. The point was they weren't going to find him today.

Valerie completed her usual patrol shift.

They rolled through the neighborhood where they had first seen Murke, stopping at Linda Seville's empty house. Maybe the older woman was out of town.

As they stepped around from the house, Valerie suggested, "We might be able to catch up with Leroy Seville through his parole officer."

Trevor nodded, unable to let go of his frustration. "That would be the next step." Squaring his shoulders, he ambled toward his car.

Once he was behind the wheel, Valerie commented, "Both times today Murke was trying to get some food, and we kept him from eating." She rested her head against the back of the seat. "Maybe we'll just starve him out."

Trevor laughed. He appreciated her being

able to find humor in the situation, but Murke was still on the run. "I thought Murke would skip town after he saw us this morning. Wonder what's keeping him here, risking being caught?"

Valerie shook her head. "You said he lived here when he was a teenager?"

"Yeah, and he's come back more than once," Trevor said.

"My brother David works undercover. He's in touch with some of the shadier people around Sagebrush. He might know something."

So her brother was a cop, too. "I'd like to talk to him."

"We're having a family barbecue tonight. You're welcome to come."

Social gatherings really weren't his thing, but he was anxious to heat up the trail that led to Murke. After all, there would be no justice for Cory Smith's death until Murke was caught. "I might do that."

She let out a heavy sigh and stared at the ceiling. "I can't wait to get out of this uniform. I smell like an Italian restaurant."

He drove across town and parked in front of her house. The patrol car that was supposed to be her off-duty protection hadn't shown up yet. He raced around to her side of the car and helped her out. He stayed close to her as they crossed the street. As close as he could get with Lexi between them.

In a lot of ways, she was a good cop, even if she was a rookie. "I appreciate the work you did today. How did you know Murke was on that side of the street?"

They came to her door. "I thought it would be better if I got out of the car and was ready for him." She looked up at him without blinking, her green eyes bright and clear. "I know you told me to stay in the car, but sitting on the sidelines is not what a cop does."

The expression on her face sent a charge through him. "You showed good instincts," he murmured.

"Thank you." When she smiled, her freckles seemed more intense.

The glow of appreciation in her voice made his heart leap.

She leaned toward him. "Guess I'll see you later for the barbecue."

"I'm not going anywhere. Your night watch isn't here yet. I'll be parked right along the curb."

"I appreciate that." She opened the door and slipped inside.

As the door eased shut, he could hear the sound of Mrs. Witherspoon's fussing over Valerie, Bethany's gleeful cry and Valerie exclaiming, "There's my girl."

Trevor returned to his car and settled in. He had some calls he needed to make. He scanned the neighborhood, which was a mixture of apartment buildings and single-family homes. Things looked pretty settled, but that didn't mean he could let his guard down. Twice Lexi came to the window and looked out at him, resting her paws on the windowsill.

That dog just didn't know what to make of him.

As he pulled his laptop out and worked through the late afternoon, he found himself looking forward to the barbecue and being with Valerie. What was it about her that was getting under his skin?

FIVE

As she slipped into a purple sundress and contemplated whether to wear her hair up or down, Valerie realized she was making choices with Trevor's reaction in mind.

"Why should I care what he thinks, huh, Lex?"

The dog, who had positioned herself by the bedroom door, tilted her chunky square head sideways as though she understood what Valerie was saying.

"It's not like I don't have enough going on already." She turned away from the full-length mirror to the bed where Bethany was propped against some pillows. The toddler broke out in a grin and then lifted the blanket to hide her face.

"Oh peek-a-boo to you, too." She swept

Bethany in her arms as the little girl let out a giggle. She bounced her up and down, making her laugh even more.

Lexi came to attention. The dog had been around Bethany at family gatherings. As Kathleen neared the end of her life, Bethany had stayed at Valerie's quite a bit, but the dog still didn't quite know what to make of this new little person in the house. She showed neither animosity nor affection for the toddler.

Valerie sat Bethany back on the bed and smoothed her troll-doll hair. She retrieved a plastic barrette from the bathroom and placed it in Bethany's blond hair. Bethany fingered the barrette but didn't pull it out. "Now we both look pretty. And we're ready to have a good time." The ache in her heart returned. She stroked Bethany's soft cheek as thoughts of Kathleen returned.

The barbecue had been her father's idea, a way of bringing the family together under more positive circumstances since Kathleen's funeral over a month ago. She understood her father's way of coping, but the cloud of sorrow would be there no matter what.

Valerie grabbed a light sweater as a cover-up. Spring evenings could still be a little chilly. She juggled Bethany, her purse and the diaper bag as she headed toward the door. Lexi followed dutifully behind.

Once outside, the cool March air greeted her. She contemplated how she was going to get her keys out of her purse to lock the door with everything she was holding.

A car door slammed and Trevor strode toward her. "Let me give you a hand."

She caught the moment of head-to-toe assessment he did of her before he spoke. A warm smile brightened his tanned face.

"Thank you." She handed him the diaper bag and placed Bethany in his arms before opening her purse to dig for her keys. "I thought we should take separate cars. I'm sure you need to get back to the hotel or wherever you're staying. The night shift protection will be in place by the time I…" She looked up at him. Bethany sucked on his shirt collar and then patted his chest three times. Trevor stiffened his shoulders. "Babies aren't quite your thing, are they?"

Color rose up in his face. "I just haven't been around them much."

She placed the key in the lock and twisted it before turning to face him. "You never had any little sisters or brothers?"

"No, it was just me." He broke off eye contact.

She had a feeling there was more to the story than he was willing to tell. She'd seen a flash of sadness or maybe it was pain in his eyes. Trevor Lewis was a hard man to figure out. She took Bethany out of his arms.

He held on to the diaper bag. "That's your car over there?"

"Yes," she said.

"It's been parked out here all day. Why don't I take a good look at it before you get in?"

Valerie's breath caught as apprehension returned. She hadn't even thought of the possibility of a bomb being planted. She wouldn't put it past the syndicate, though.

Trevor opened and closed doors, ran his hands underneath seats, searched the trunk and checked the underside of the car. He rose to his feet and dusted off his pants. "Take it slow. I'll follow behind you."

Valerie placed Bethany in her car seat in the back, and Lexi took her position in the passenger seat. As they drove, Lexi alerted to the movement of people and cars on the street. Like any good cop, there wasn't much that the dog didn't notice.

Valerie checked her rearview mirror. Trevor's sedan remained close. They passed the Lost Woods before arriving at a suburb on the outskirts of Sagebrush.

Valerie had pulled Bethany out of her car seat by the time Trevor rolled in behind her in the driveway. He got out of his car and flashed her a quick smile. "We made it."

Her stomach fluttered when he looked at her with those dark, intense eyes. What was it about this guy that stirred up these feelings of attraction? "Come on, let's go meet my family."

Trevor followed Valerie around the side of the house as he took in his surroundings. He hadn't wanted to tell Valerie, to ruin her evening out with her family, but he was pretty sure they'd been followed.

The chatter of voices and water splashing in a pool greeted him even before he saw the huge crowd gathered on the patio. An older man in a Hawaiian shirt flipped burgers while he spoke to a woman in a wheelchair. Young children jumped in the pool and came out shivering. Adults milled in and out of the house or sat at a patio table. He estimated that there were at least ten adults and just as many children.

Valerie leaned close to him. "Don't be

intimidated. Not all of them are family—
some are friends and neighbors."

A woman with long, blond hair came
up to Valerie and held out her arms for
Bethany. "There's my sweet baby."

"Trevor, this is Lucy Cullen. We met
when I was assigned protective duty for
her."

Lucy gathered Bethany into her arms.
"And we've been friends ever since."

"She's engaged to a fellow K-9 officer."
Valerie pointed across the pool at a tall,
muscular man with light brown hair. "Lee
Calloway."

Lucy's gaze fell on Trevor. "I'll watch
Bethany for a while. Why don't you relax
and enjoy yourself." She sauntered away
holding Bethany.

Valerie set the diaper bag down. "My
brother David should be around here
somewhere." She scanned the crowd. "I'll
have you meet my dad first."

She took his hand as though it were the
most natural thing in the world and led
him toward the man by the barbecue. The

softness of her grip sent a surge of heat through him.

She let go of his hand and touched his shoulder. "Dad, this is Agent Trevor Lewis from the San Antonio FBI. We're working together to catch a fugitive."

The older man put his spatula down and offered Trevor a hardy handshake. "Detective Ben Salgado, retired, twenty-five years on the force."

Trevor nodded. "Appreciate your service, sir."

Ben offered him a wide grin. "Trying to talk Valerie into taking the detective's exam. Once she gets done with this dog thing."

Valerie turned slightly and bent her head, staring at her feet. "I enjoy the K-9 unit."

The moment passed quickly, but he had caught a tremor in her voice that suggested hurt.

Oblivious to how his comment had affected his daughter, Ben flipped a burger and then turned to face them again. "This is my wife, Helen." Ben pointed toward the woman in the wheelchair, who nodded.

"I worked dispatch until this muscular disease got the better of me. Ben and I met when we were both employed by the police department." Salt and pepper hair framed Helen Salgado's slender face. Kind eyes looked at him from behind wire-rimmed glasses.

"Daddy, we're looking for David. Where is he?"

"Mary and the girls came separately. David is still on duty. He should be here any minute," Helen said.

Ben slapped Trevor's back. "In the meantime, have a burger. Drinks and sides are over by the table."

While Trevor ate, Valerie retrieved Bethany from Lucy only to have her taken away again by a gray-haired grandmotherly woman. Trevor took a bite of his burger and watched the action around him.

Lexi sat where Valerie had commanded

her to stay. Though children would come by to pet her, she remained stoic and vigilant, always watching. When one of the kids had pointed a plastic water pistol at Valerie, Lexi had stirred to her feet, waiting for the command from Valerie to attack. Valerie had given her a hand signal that told her it was okay to lie down.

That was something he had in common with the dog. He'd never been much of a mixer at social gatherings, preferring to remain on the perimeter as an observer.

Valerie walked around the other picnic tables, grabbing the empty plates. The setting sun gave her skin a luminescent quality and her long, red hair had shaken loose from the ponytail. He jumped up when she headed back toward the house with a stack of dirty plates. Maybe that car hadn't been following them on the way in, but he didn't want to take any chance of her being alone or vulnerable. He could stay close without her having to think about the death threat.

He caught up with Valerie just as she

placed the dishes in the sink. Her back was turned toward him. The big windows provided too much of an opportunity for Valerie to be seen. It would be nothing for a sniper to fire a shot through them.

They were alone in the kitchen, the noise from the party outside muffled by the patio door. "Why don't we go back to the yard?"

Startled, Valerie turned and placed her palm on her chest. "I didn't realize you'd followed me in." Evening light streaming through kitchen windows washed over her. "I just needed to get away from all the noise for a moment and catch my breath. I kind of like the quiet."

After seeing how shaken up she was from the email threat at the station, he felt the need to protect her not just physically, but emotionally, too. She needed to have a nice night with her family and not have to think about the ever-watchful eyes of the syndicate. "I just think we should get back. I'm sure Bethany is missing you."

She laughed, a soft trilling sound. "I

don't think I am going to get that baby back until the night is over."

Headlights created shadows across the living room carpet. Someone was pulling up the street by the Salgado's long driveway.

"Oh, I bet that's David." She rushed through the kitchen toward the entryway and flung open the door.

Trevor followed on her heels, as the evening air chilled his skin.

She ran halfway down the long driveway. He could just make out the outline of the car he had seen earlier.

A man covered in shadows got out of the car.

"David!" she waved.

Trevor caught up with Valerie and wrapped his arm around her shoulder. "Let's go back inside."

She resisted when he tried to guide her back to the house. "What are you talking about?"

The man stopped, then pivoted and returned to the car.

She tensed. "That wasn't my brother."

"No," he said, pulling her close.

"They followed us here. They…they know where my parents live." Her voice faltered and she began to tremble.

He drew her close. "I don't know for sure. Maybe that guy was just lost." She rested her face against his chest. He covered her with his arms and held her until the shaking stopped. Her back expanded and contracted with the steady intake and exhale of her breath.

She pulled back and tilted her head toward him. "I forgot. For just one moment, I forgot that my life was in danger."

"We can't take any chances." He'd do anything to give her back a normal life, but that wasn't within his power. All he could do was protect her and watch over her. "Come on, let's go back to the party."

"What do you suppose that man's plan was?" Fear still permeated her words.

He stayed close to her as they turned to go back inside. "If it was the syndicate, he was probably going to scope out…an opportunity." They walked across the living room floor.

"There's lots of trees around the backyard to hide in. I'm sure he would have found—" she cleared her throat "—a place to hide and get a clean shot."

For now, Trevor's presence had deterred the would-be assassin.

She opened the patio door and the happy noises of the party spilled into the living room. She hesitated at the door, her mouth drawn into a pensive line.

He placed a supportive hand on the middle of her back, leaned close and whispered in her ear. "I know it feels like you can't ever relax because of this. Just know that I'm here."

Mr. Salgado waved at them from a close picnic table. "David's here." He pointed across the pool at a man with long hair sitting in a lawn chair.

"He must have pulled around back because the driveway was full of cars," Valerie said as she stepped outside.

David Salgado pulled his sunglasses off

and stood up as Valerie and Trevor approached. He was at least ten years older than Valerie. The long hair was probably part of his undercover work.

"David, this is Agent Trevor Lewis from San Antonio. He's trying to track down a man named Derek Murke." Valerie had a faraway look in her eyes. She was probably still rattled by what had happened in the driveway.

David rubbed his forehead. "Derek Murke. Yeah, I remember him. He was robbing convenience stores when I was still on patrol."

"He's back in town. You have any idea where he might be?" Trevor asked. "He's probably worn out his welcome with his old partner in crime, Leroy Seville, and the aunt he was staying with."

David made a clicking sound with his tongue. "Murke did a lot of petty thievery."

"He graduated up to armed robbery about two years ago," Trevor said.

David rubbed his chin. "Seems like he

had a half sister. She had a different last name than him, much more law abiding, too. I'm sure I could track down the name for you."

"Thanks, I'd appreciate that." Trevor slapped David's back and shook his hand before handing him a business card. "Give me a call when you know."

"Will do."

Valerie came up beside him and touched his forearm lightly. "Trevor, I think I'm ready to go home. I don't like the idea of putting my family in danger." Her voice had a pleading quality.

Trevor nodded. "I don't blame you."

As they walked away, David said, "I'll let you know as soon as I remember. Take care of my sister."

He helped Valerie gather up Bethany and the baby's things. David's words echoed in his brain. More than anything, he wanted to keep her safe.

Valerie gave him a backward glance before commanding Lexi to come.

"I'll follow you home," he said. "We

need to make sure your night protection is in place."

She nodded, but didn't say anything. He waited for her on the quiet suburban street while she backed out of the driveway. He remained close as they made their way back to town through the city streets to her home. The red glare of her taillights overshadowed the outline of her head and of Lexi's head in the passenger seat.

She slowed when she got close to her house. The police car was already parked outside. Trevor pulled in behind her. He waved at the police officer and followed Valerie up to her door. She had removed the car seat with the sleeping Bethany in it. Valerie fumbled in her purse for her keys. She pushed open the door.

"Why don't you let me have a look around inside first?"

Again, she nodded. He checked both her first and second floor as well as the backyard. Satisfied, he returned to where she waited in the foyer. "All clear." He squeezed her shoulder. "Have a good night."

He waited outside until he heard the lock click into place. He recognized the police officer from the station this morning. The man rolled down his window as Trevor approached. He leaned on the window. "Keep her safe."

"You got it," said the officer.

He got in his car and drove away. He circled the block twice before finally feeling like he could let go. He wanted to stay there all night, to watch over her. But he would be no good to anyone if he didn't get some sleep.

As he hopped on the freeway to head to the hotel, the lights of the city stretched before him. He had always thought there was something comforting about a city at night viewed from a distance. The twinkling lights and the silence masked all of the turmoil taking place on the streets and in some homes at night.

Valerie had a family that loved her and Bethany. She had siblings who cared about her. The whole experience had been surreal to him. He had grown up in a home where all the happy families who cared about each other were on television. Valerie wouldn't want anything to do with him if she knew what kind of family he came from...what his father had done to his mother.

He spotted a sign for the hotel and hit the blinker. Why did she matter so much to him if he couldn't see himself fitting into her life? He went to the hotel room he'd checked into the previous night. The room was clean, but the silence stood in sharp contrast to the chatter of the barbecue earlier. As he tossed his suitcase on the bed and pulled off his jacket, he was struck by a profound loneliness.

Valerie woke in the night to the sensation of Lexi licking her fingers. The room was dark except for a night-light close to Bethany's bed.

"What is it?" Valerie whispered.

Lexi whined.

Bethany stirred in her crib, but luckily she didn't wake up.

Valerie threw back the covers and followed Lexi to the main floor. She checked Lexi's food and water dish, though the dog was not in the habit of waking her for something so trivial. Maybe she was just restless.

Valerie flicked on the faucet and grabbed a cup. When she had finished her water, the dog hadn't settled down. Valerie checked that the police car was still parked outside and all the doors were locked. She returned to the kitchen. Lexi stood at attention by the patio door.

Valerie's hands were clammy as she reached to open the blinds on the glass of the patio door. She hesitated, gripping the string for the blinds. The truth was she didn't want to see what was outside. She didn't want to see a stranger with a gun pointed at her. Or the Serpent's yellow eyes burning through her. Or Derek Murke's face compressed into an expression of hate.

As a cop, she had faced danger before. She'd had guns pointed at her. But this wasn't about a criminal wanting to avoid jail time. This was personal. The syndicate wanted her dead. That took her fear to a whole new level.

As blood thrummed in her ears and she struggled for a deep breath, she found the courage to open the blinds all the way. Dark shadows and movement caused her to take a step back. Lexi came up beside her and leaned against her. She stroked the dog's head, an action that calmed both of them.

"What do you think is out there?" She could not clearly discern anything outside. Maybe someone had been in the yard and maybe it was just her heightened state of awareness. Valerie closed the blinds, and Lexi finally relaxed.

She trudged upstairs. She hovered over Bethany's crib until she heard the soft sound of Bethany's breathing. Assured that the baby was okay, she crawled beneath her covers and pulled her legs up to her stomach.

Seeing the police car outside did ease some of her fear, but she couldn't help but think that she would feel even safer if it was Trevor who was parked outside.

SIX

Captain Slade McNeal strode toward Valerie's desk looking like a man on a mission. Judging from the tightness of his expression, either her paperwork was messed up or he had something very serious for her to do.

She checked the entrance to the K-9 administrative area. Still no sign of Trevor. She'd called him early in the morning, and they'd agreed to meet at the station. Her night duty protection had followed her into the station. She'd looked at Derek Murke's criminal file again but didn't find a mention of a half sister. Hopefully, David would remember the woman's name.

McNeal stopped a few feet from her

desk. "Salgado, I just got a call. A group of school children found a dog matching Rio's description collapsed underneath a bush in Palo Verde Park." Though McNeal never gave much away in terms of emotion, there was intensity in his piercing blue eyes that Valerie had not seen before.

Valerie jumped to her feet. "I'll go with you." Rio had been missing since January. If this was McNeal's dog, the whole department would breathe a collective sigh of relief.

Lexi stood up and looked to Valerie, waiting for a command. Her bobbed tail vibrated in anticipation. "Lex, come."

Trevor was just pulling into the back parking lot as they headed toward the patrol car. He was clean shaven and the light blue windbreaker he wore set off his dark hair and eyes. His smile drew her in.

Trevor glanced from McNeal to Valerie. "Something going on?"

"I've got to take this call at Palo Verde

Park." She looked over her shoulder at McNeal. "It's important."

McNeal put a hand on her shoulder. "She'll be all right. She'll be with me."

"I got in touch with Leroy Seville's parole officer. He's got an appointment this morning. It's a chance for me to find out what Murke said to him…if anything," Trevor said. "I can meet you at the park after the interview."

As Trevor returned to his car and pulled out of the lot, Valerie and McNeal rushed to the patrol car, putting Lexi in the back. Captain McNeal radioed the animal warden to meet them at the park. If this was Rio, there was no telling what condition the dog would be in. The syndicate could have beaten him and left him for dead. Or the dog might have become vicious due to mistreatment.

As she drove, Valerie glanced over at her captain. Deep furrows through his forehead indicated his level of anxiety. He touched his dark hair where it was graying at the temple, a gesture that gave away how nervous he was. The burden he had carried since Rio's disappearance had been a heavy one. Not only had he lost his dog, but Slade's dad had also been badly beaten during the abduction. Valerie had heard that he was on the mend, though. On top of everything, Rio had been a best friend and protector to Slade's five-year-old son, Caleb, since the boy's mom had died.

Her heart went out to Slade. He needed some morsel of hope. "Maybe this will be it. Maybe we found him, huh?"

"If it is him, collapsed on a playground is not a good sign." His voice faltered, betraying the level of worry he must be going through. McNeal shifted slightly in his seat. "How are things working out with Agent Lewis?"

McNeal didn't want to talk about Rio, so he'd changed the subject. Though he was a man who kept his emotions in check, Valerie had seen the sorrow over the loss rise to the surface in subtle ways. The loss of a K-9 partner stung as much as if Rio had been human. The dogs were officers and partners in every way. She never doubted that Lexi had her back and would take a bullet for her. She understood about him not wanting to talk about it. "How well did you say you knew Agent Lewis?"

"We've done joint training exercises together." McNeal stared out the window.

Valerie hit the blinker and made the turn into the park. "He's a competent agent. He's a little bit closed down when it comes to sharing much about himself, though."

McNeal nodded but didn't offer any further information. Knowing something about where a person had come from was probably not important to a man. Connection to people, getting to know them, was everything to her. She'd worked at building the trust of the people in the neighborhoods she patrolled and with all the people in her life.

As they pulled into the parking lot, fatigue mixed with the anticipation she felt about finding Rio. She'd only had half a cup of coffee. Not only had Lexi awakened her in the night, but Bethany had stood up in her crib only a few hours after Valerie had gone back to sleep, clinging tightly to the worn pink bunny. It just seemed like Bethany should have fallen into a less restless pattern of sleep by now. Valerie worried that she wasn't comforting and holding Bethany enough. And then she worried that she was holding her too much. She really didn't know what she was doing when it came to being Bethany's mom. Kathleen had been such a natural. Sometimes she wondered why her sister had had so much confidence in her.

When they arrived at the park, Valerie commanded Lexi to follow her. As they got out of the patrol car and headed across the long stretch of grass to the playground, the ache over Kathleen's loss returned. Grief rose to the surface at the strangest times.

I just don't know if I can be a good mom.

A group of children along with a woman who must be their teacher stood by the playground equipment. Valerie could make out the prone body of a German shepherd beneath the bushes.

"Let's approach with caution. We don't know what he's been through." McNeal was already thinking that the dog was Rio.

The teacher came toward them with the children trailing behind her. "I'm Mrs. Scott—we're the ones who phoned in."

One of the children, a girl of about six dressed in a pink polka-dot coat, peeked around Mrs. Scott. "The dog growled at us and then cried out like he wasn't feeling good."

"If you could just stay back," McNeal advised and then looked around. "Where's the animal warden?"

"I'm sure Robert's on his way," Valerie said, turning her attention toward the dog.

"We can't wait for him. Let's just move in slowly and see if we can figure out what is going on with the dog." McNeal's voice was thick with emotion.

Valerie dropped to the ground and approached the dog. Captain McNeal took the lead, and Valerie inched behind him. From this angle, she couldn't see any obvious injuries on the dog. The dog lifted its head with a wary eye toward McNeal.

Valerie made soothing sounds as she eased closer. The dog was laying on what looked like a child's coat and a picnic blanket.

"There, boy," said McNeal.

The dog raised its head and growled. McNeal stopped, unable to hide his anguish. His eyebrows pinched together.

"She doesn't like men. Some dogs are like that." Mrs. Scott had come up behind them.

"Ma'am, please, I'm going to have to ask you to stand back." Valerie knew McNeal well enough to know that the harshness of his tone was not meant for Mrs. Scott. That the dog had growled at the sound of McNeal's voice was not a good sign. Either Rio had been so traumatized that the bond between handler and dog had been broken, or this dog was not Rio.

McNeal patted Valerie's shoulder. "Go ahead and move in."

Valerie scooted closer. The dog lifted her head and whimpered. It took Valerie only a minute to see blood on the tail and the canine's bulb-like stomach. Valerie closed her eyes in disappointment. "Captain, this isn't Rio. This dog is about to have pups."

Repeated gleeful cries of, "Puppies! Puppies! She's going to have puppies," came from the children.

Mrs. Scott shushed the children and scooted them farther back.

"She's nesting. That's why she dragged that coat and that blanket over here." Valerie turned to look at her boss.

His features were distorted from despair for only a moment before he recovered. "The right thing to do here is to help that dog have her pups and make sure we get her transported to a safe place."

"Yes, sir." Valerie turned her attention back toward the dog. She reached a tentative hand toward the dog's head. The dog whined and stiffened in pain from a contraction. Empathy surged through Valerie's body. "It's all right." She soothed the dog's head.

There were no tags or collar. The dog looked thin but not malnourished. She heard footsteps behind her and turned to see Robert Cane.

Though she addressed the animal warden, she kept her tone soothing so as not to agitate the dog. "She's not crazy about men."

"I'll just hang back here, Valerie. It looks like you're doing fine," said Robert.

The dog closed her eyes and panted. "But I'm not trained for this," Valerie said.

"She'll do most of the work." She could hear Robert repositioning himself behind her. "I can watch from here and let you know if you need to intervene."

Valerie took in a deep breath, hoping to ease the tension in her neck and back. "So I guess it's up to me."

"You got a new job title, Valerie—canine midwife." Slade's voice came from a few feet behind her.

His joking didn't quite hide the undertone of sorrow she picked up in his voice. The man missed his dog, not just for him but for his kid, also.

The first four pups came quickly. The mother licked off the protective air sack of each. With their eyes still closed, they grunted and pushed until they found a nipple to nurse on. A fifth puppy emerged, but did not move. The mother was still occupied cleaning the fourth puppy.

Valerie's hands became clammy. "He's not moving, Robert. This little guy isn't moving."

"He needs to get air into his lungs. Hold him upside down and swing him like a golf club," the animal warden said.

"*What?*"

"I know it sounds crazy, Valerie, but it works."

Valerie picked up the motionless slimy black body and did as Robert instructed. The puppy still showed no signs of life.

Please, God, don't let this little guy die.

Robert's soft voice didn't conceal his concern. Tension strung through his words. "Try again."

She swung the pup one more time… and waited. The pup let out a noise that sounded like a sneeze and wiggled to life.

Valerie let out the breath she'd been holding. Behind her, she heard the collective sigh of the school children. The puppy moved more vigorously in her hands.

"You're a natural." Robert edged toward her. "Now put her close to the mother so they can bond."

Valerie placed the squirming pup close to the mother's nose. The dog lifted her head and licked the black fur. The instinct to nurture seemed to come easily

to the female shepherd. A deeper understanding stirred inside Valerie. Maybe
she needed to trust her own maternal instincts where Bethany was concerned. As
hard as it was, Valerie couldn't imagine
her life without that little girl. She wasn't
going to be a perfect mom, but she'd be
the best mom she could be for Bethany.

Once the mother dog was done cleaning the pup, Valerie placed him close to
the mother's belly so he could nurse. The
little pup was smaller than the others, but
fought his way to the top of the pile.

Robert came up behind her. The female dog lifted her head but didn't growl.
"That little guy has some strong survival
instincts."

Valerie nodded. "I suppose we should
leave mother and babies alone." She
rose to her feet and stood beside Robert.
"We'll have to transport her and the pups
when she's ready."

"We'll find homes for them when they
are old enough," Robert said.

McNeal came and stood beside them.

"Maybe the mother would be a good candidate for the K-9 training program."

A blond girl broke away from the group of children watching at a distance. She looped her fingers through the straps of her purple backpack and looked up at Valerie. "Can we see them now?"

"I suppose that would be okay." Valerie looked toward Robert for guidance.

"Just a couple of kids at a time, and you can't touch them," he advised.

The little girl nodded.

Valerie stepped back toward the bushes. The school girl kneeled beside her. Her eyes grew wide when Valerie lifted the branches for a view of the nursing pups. "Wow."

Mama dog licked one of the wayward pups and scooted it back toward the warmth of her tummy and the litter with her nose.

"She takes good care of them," the little girl said. "How does she know what to do?"

"It's just the way God made her. She's wired to be a mom," Valerie said.

They kneeled for a moment watching the pups, some sleeping and others still probing for an opportunity to nurse more. The little girl's hand slipped into Valerie's. She held the warm little hand in her own as though it were as fragile as a snowflake. Bethany would do this in time, and she relished the opportunity to share the wonder of birth with her daughter. Yes, that was it. Bethany was *her daughter* now.

They backed away from the bushes. "Now," said Valerie, "go get three more of your friends and tell them to come over here."

Valerie ushered over groups of two and three children until McNeal tapped her on the shoulder.

"Your partner is here," he said.

Trevor stood by the edge of the swing set some distance from the children.

"I'll finish up here and take Agent Lewis's car back to the station. I know you need to do your regular patrol—Robert can make sure the dog is safe," McNeal assured her.

The school children chimed as she walked by them, "Goodbye, Officer Salgado."

Valerie waved at them before turning to face Trevor. She couldn't read his expression but something about him seemed… softer. She wasn't quite sure what had caused the change. Had he been watching the drama of the puppies being born for some time?

"So McNeal tells me the dog wasn't Rio and now the department has five puppies to deal with," Trevor said as he walked beside Valerie.

Valerie commanded Lexi to come and the dog fell in beside her. "We'll try to find the owner. If not, we'll see that they are placed in homes." They strolled across the stretch of lawn to the parking lot. "So did Leroy make his meeting?"

"Yeah, I'm pretty sure Murke won't be welcomed back. Leroy is working hard at going straight, and Murke wore out his welcome when he took Leroy's Buick." He gazed down at her. "The aunt is out of town for a month or more. When Leroy got out of prison, she said he could house sit. If Murke does show up, I'm sure Leroy will give us a call."

Valerie let Lexi into the backseat of the patrol car. "That's good news. So do you think Murke has left town?"

"I don't know." Trevor got into the passenger seat. "Your brother called me with the name of Murke's half sister. I thought we'd go over there and try to talk to her."

Valerie settled in, started the car and turned around. While she waited for a car to pass by before pulling out into the street, she studied the hard lines and angles of Trevor's face.

He offered her a glance with a smile that was more of a spasm. Something was going on with him.

"So everything was pretty routine this morning?"

He tapped his fingers on the dashboard. "Yeah, sure, why?"

"I don't know. You just seemed different when you were standing in the park… like you were thinking about something," Valerie said.

He picked up a small notebook from the cup holder. "That's the address where Murke's half sister lives. Her name is Crystal."

He was good at changing the subject. She took the piece of paper and read the address while stopped at an intersection. "I know where this is." She sped through the intersection. "So what were you thinking about in the park?" If they were going to work together, she wanted to know more about him. He certainly hadn't revealed anything personal to McNeal.

His eye twitched. "Who says I was thinking about anything?"

She caught the defensiveness in his tone. She focused her attention on the view through the windshield. The car clicked past a mall and some big-box stores. Why did it even matter to her that she wanted to know more about him…to see more of the man underneath that thick exterior?

The silence in the car became oppressive. Valerie rolled down the window, letting the spring breeze caress her face. Lexi leaned over her shoulder to take in the outdoor smells.

"Not every family is like your family, you know," Trevor blurted.

She picked up on just a slight waver in his voice. If she hadn't had interview and interrogation training, she'd never have noticed it. His comment had come out of left field. She wasn't sure where this was leading.

"I think the street is just up here a ways." She took in a breath and glanced over at him. "What do you mean not every family is like mine?"

"You got people that love you and care about you," Trevor said. "They want your career to turn out right, and they help you with Bethany."

"Yes, that's true." She still wasn't sure what he was implying.

His gaze shifted more than was necessary. This wasn't easy for him, whatever he was trying to say. Slowing down as they entered a residential neighborhood, she parked the car outside the house where Murke's half sister lived. Then she looked over at him, waiting for an explanation.

Valerie's gaze was like a heavy weight on him. Sweat trickled down his neck. Now he regretted even breaching the subject of his family. Talking about them was harder than sniper duty in below-zero weather.

She'd run to the hills when she knew what kind of family he'd come from. He'd grown up in a home that half the time didn't have electricity because his father didn't pay the bill. His mom had tried to make the house a home. She had tried until…that night.

"So you're saying your family isn't like

mine." She leaned closer. Her green eyes intense as the scent of her perfume enveloped him.

He liked the way she tried to make it easier for him. It loosened some of the tension that was like a cord twisting around his chest. When he had watched her at a distance with the children and the puppies, he'd felt a longing to be a part of the tender moment she had created. That was what had started this whole thing. He didn't want to be the outsider anymore.

"How bad could it be? My family isn't perfect, either." Her eyes seemed to probe beneath his skin straight to his heart. "I wish my dad would get off my case about the detective exam."

She had no idea. He braced his hands on the dashboard and delivered his words in rapid fire intensity. "Your father never murdered your mother."

Valerie's eyes widened and her mouth dropped open as a look of shock and then horror spread across her face.

The comment had come out all wrong.

He said it like he was trying to push her away with his words. And maybe that was what he had intended. Her openness and her sweetness enticed and frightened him at the same time. His stomach felt like it was in knots. Why did he push her away when what he wanted more than anything was to draw her close?

He couldn't look at her. For sure now, she wouldn't want anything to do with him. He opened the door. He should just do what he was good at—work. They had an interview to conduct. He could hear her footsteps behind him as he strode up the sidewalk and pounded on the door.

He couldn't bring himself to look her in the eye when they stood on the porch waiting for someone to come to the door.

A boy of about five wearing a T-shirt that hung down below his knees answered the door. The kid had the telltale signs of having eaten a peanut butter sandwich, a smear of grape jelly at the corners of his mouth.

"Is your mom home?"

The little boy led them through the house to the backyard where a woman was placing plants in a flower bed. Crystal Stern was a plump woman with brassy blond hair held back by a scarf. She looked to be in her late thirties. She assessed Valerie's uniform and asked, "Is this about Derek?"

"So you've been in contact with him?" Trevor said.

The little boy lingered by the door until Crystal commanded, "Taylor go on inside and finish your lunch."

Taylor made a noise of protest but turned and marched inside.

"My boy doesn't need to hear any more about his wayward uncle." Crystal looked up at them, shading her eyes from the sun. "I don't want anything to do with that man. Any nice thing he does is just a setup to take advantage of me."

Trevor cleared his throat. "Ma'am, he's wanted for armed robbery and killing an agent in Arizona. If we can catch him, we can put him away for a long time."

Crystal picked up another plant and turned it upside down. She dug a hole with her trowel. She was probably mulling over what he had said, debating her options.

Trevor glanced over at Valerie who seemed to understand that it was better to remain silent. Give the woman time to think.

Crystal let out a heavy sigh and placed her hand on her hip. "He was here yesterday. Came by with a new toy for Taylor and a bunch of promises I know he won't keep."

"I take it he didn't stay here last night?"

"No. He wanted to. Said he was going to come into 'a big score.'" Crystal made quotation marks with her fingers. "He said he could get it in the next few days and that it was easy money no one could touch."

Valerie shifted her weight. "Those were his exact words—'easy money no one can touch?'"

"Pretty much. And he wanted his father's old gun, which I wasn't about to give him." Crystal wiped the sweat from her brow with the back of her hand.

So Murke was looking for a gun. Could the score he talked about be another robbery? "Did he say anything else?"

"He said he could pay me rent once he got this score." She blew out a puff of air that made her lips vibrate. "Trust me, I heard it all before where Derek is concerned. He's the king of the broken promises. I've waited my whole life for him to act like a real big brother."

Trevor tried to keep his conversation casual, though he felt a sense of excitement. The trail to Murke was heating up. "Any idea where he might have gone?"

She shook her head. "Derek is a master manipulator. I'm sure he'll find somebody to take him in. I don't think he has much money."

Valerie glanced around the yard. "So do you think this big score he talked about is why he came back into town?"

Crystal exhaled slowly. "Actually, he

said something about getting even with an old girlfriend who double-crossed him years ago."

Valerie shifted her weight. "Do you know the name of this woman?"

Crystal shrugged. "Derek left Sagebrush when he was eighteen. He's been back a couple of times, but I'm not able to keep track of all the girlfriends he's had over the years. Quite frankly, I try to associate with him as little as possible."

She pulled off her garden gloves and assessed her fingernails. "I can tell you one thing. Whoever she is, he's plenty mad at her. He all but spit venom when he talked about getting back at her."

"You sure he didn't say a first or last name?" Valerie asked, stepping toward Crystal.

"The name he called her is not fit to be spoken, if you know what I mean." Crystal turned and wandered toward a small shed at the back of the yard. "That's all I got to tell you. You can let yourself out through the side gate."

As they strolled toward the side of the yard, Trevor could see Taylor with his face pressed against the sliding glass door. Something about the kid reminded him of himself at that age. A lonely boy making peanut butter sandwiches and watching cartoons.

Once inside the patrol car, the uncomfortable silence settled between them like an oppressive fog. Lexi whined in the backseat as though she had picked up on the mood. Trevor clenched his teeth. All he had to do was apprehend Murke and leave town. Why did he feel this need for Valerie to know the ugliness of his childhood?

Valerie offered him a faint smile. "So what do you suppose the big score is that Derek told Crystal about?"

He had tensed for a moment when she had looked at him, fearing she would want to resume the conversation where they'd left off. He had probably shocked her so badly, she wouldn't want to know anything more about his private life. "Hard to say. Since his specialty is robbery, it sounds like he's looking for a gun. It's interesting that he said it was money no one could touch."

Valerie nodded. "That caught me, too, like he was talking about money that was obtained illegally in the first place or laundered."

Valerie rolled through a middle-class neighborhood. She glanced over at Trevor and then focused her attention straight ahead. She pulled the car over to the curb and turned to face him. "I don't know exactly what happened between your mom and dad, but it wasn't right to put a kid through that." She shook her head as tears formed at the corners of her eyes. "That sort of thing is never right. Never."

Warmth pooled around Trevor's heart. She wasn't crying for him. She was crying for the twelve-year-old kid who had come home and found his mother dead. He swallowed the lump in his throat. "It's over now. It's the past."

She held his gaze even as a tear flowed

down her cheek. "No one would ever know that about you by meeting you today."

"I had some help along the way. Good foster homes. A pastor who loved me like a son." He reached over and brushed the tear off her cheek with his thumb. All the shame of the past fell away with her acceptance of him, of where he had come from.

She placed her hand over his. With her hand warming his, he felt closer to her than he had ever felt with anyone. Her green eyes held such depth of compassion.

The female voice of the dispatcher came through the radio, causing both of them to jump. "K-9 Unit 349, we have a domestic in progress at the end of Wilshire. House number 787."

Valerie picked up the radio. "Copy. We are about five blocks from that location."

Dispatch continued to relay information as they drove. A neighbor had phoned in when the squabble had escalated.

Valerie sped up as she merged into traffic. Sensing the excitement, Lexi twirled in circles in the backseat and let out yipping sounds. The car motor revved in time to the pounding of Trevor's heart.

The moment between them had been broken by the reality of her job, but he would not be the same after this. She had not run when he had revealed the harsh truth of his childhood.

Valerie slowed the car, nearing the address dispatch had given her. She sat up a little straighter as the worry lines on her forehead intensified.

Something was making the red flags go up for her. Trevor leaned forward in the seat. "What is it?"

SEVEN

Valerie came to a stop by the house. The hair on the back of her neck stood up. Lexi, who had ceased turning circles in the backseat, let out a single yip.

"Something wrong?" Trevor asked.

The house was one of five homes that occupied a city block. They had just passed two empty lots where houses had been torn down. On the other side of the block was an apartment building still under construction. Construction trailers, heavy equipment and materials surrounded a multi-story building that was mostly framing and scaffolding. This was a neighborhood in the midst of renewal. It looked like these were the last five old houses left.

"I'm not so sure anybody even lives here." Valerie clicked out of her seat belt and keyed the radio. "Be advised, this may be a false alarm."

There were still some signs of life in the house next door. A child's tricycle, some wilting plants in the flower bed and a car that looked like it still ran parked at the curb. The house at the end of the block had a sprinkler turned on. Signs of habitation, but still something didn't feel right.

"We still have to check it out," Trevor said.

Valerie nodded. "I'm leaving Lexi in the car. Sometimes adding a dog trained to protect to the mix of a domestic makes things worse. I can deploy her if I need to."

Trevor got out of the car and continued to survey the scene. Two blocks away, the noise of people driving up and down the street, children playing and dogs barking was muffled by distance.

Valerie approached the house with her

hand on her gun. As a patrol officer, she had to assume worst-case scenario even if things looked benign. "Sometimes the most critical moment in a domestic is when things get quiet. The man could be holding a knife or gun to his wife's throat right now."

Trevor nodded before walking across the brown lawn to assess the side of the house. He returned to her side and grabbed her elbow. "There. I saw movement by that window."

She'd seen it, too. A glimpse of a man in a sleeveless white shirt and then he'd disappeared into the darkness of the back of the house. "I'll circle around the back." She didn't give him time to protest. "You take the front."

Once at the back door, she eased it open. From the front of the house, Trevor knocked and identified himself. "Sir, we know you are in there. Please come to the door."

She waited a few minutes for the man to respond. Nothing. A musty smell hit her as she stepped into a long hallway. When she passed a child's bedroom, only a mattress and few broken toys were left on the floor. The place looked abandoned. Yet she had clearly seen someone in here.

The front door creaked open, and Trevor stepped inside.

She moved through the hallway, clearing another room and checking a closet as she moved toward the other side of the house. She heard footsteps, probably Trevor's, as he cleared the living room and the kitchen. She came to a final closed door at the side of the house. She took in a quick, sharp breath. All the other doors had been open. If the man was hiding anywhere, it had to be in here. The floorboard creaked as she eased forward and reached out for the doorknob.

She feared the worst. A woman tied up or restrained…or dead already. She twisted the knob, gripping her gun with the other hand.

The hall closet slid open and a man

caught her from behind. "Drop your gun right now."

She felt the cold hard steel of a gun barrel pressed into her temple.

Trevor had cleared the kitchen and living room, and was headed up the stairs when he heard what sounded like a scuffle at the far end of the house. He scrambled down the stairs, leaping over the railing when he was five steps from the bottom.

He checked rooms as he dashed down the hall toward a closed door and an open closet. He kicked open the door, fearing he would find Valerie on the floor in a puddle of blood. The room was empty. As he stepped outside the room, he saw her police-issue Glock dropped on the floor by the closet.

"Valerie." He took off in a dead run. The back door was flung open. He dashed outside, training his eyes on the construction site. He saw them for only a split second. The man had his arm around Valerie's neck as they disappeared behind a backhoe.

He ran the short distance to the construction site. He saw no sign of them and heard only the metal beams creaking in the wind. They could be anywhere in this labyrinth of construction materials, equipment and trailers. Clearly, this wasn't a domestic. Why had the man taken her? An icy chill filled his veins. *The syndicate.* They'd been set up.

He turned a half circle, scanning the trailers and piles of wood planks as alarm spread through him. If this man was intent on killing Valerie, Trevor had only minutes to find her. He had to be precise in his search.

He ran back around to the car, called for backup and then peered over the seat at Lexi.

"Can you help me find Valerie?"

The dog licked her chops and stepped side to side. He opened the back door of the patrol vehicle and Lexi leaped out. She looked at him as if waiting for a command. He grabbed Valerie's police hat and allowed Lexi to sniff.

"Find Valerie, find her."

He didn't know what the proper commands were. Would the dog even understand? Did she know how to track?

He pulled on her long canvas leash. "Come on, this way, Lexi." He pulled her to the back of the house by the open door where the man had exited with Valerie.

The dog kept looking at him as though waiting for clearer direction. This had to work. He couldn't wait any longer.

He waved the hat beneath her nose one more time. Lexi wagged her bobbed tail and whimpered. She was waiting for him to give her a command. "I need to find her." Desperation colored his words.

Lexi lifted her head, sniffed the air and then put her nose to the ground. She ran in circles that grew wider and wider and then bounded in the direction of the construction site. The dog had picked up on something.

He raced after her, praying that Lexi

was following the scent that would lead them to Valerie before it was too late.

Overpowered by her assailant, Valerie struggled to find an opportunity for escape. With one arm, he pressed the gun into her side. The other arm locked her neck in place. When she twisted side to side, he applied pressure to her neck, cutting off her breathing.

Images of piles of wood and steel and some kind of large moving equipment with a bucket on it flashed by her as he dragged her deeper into the construction site. She dug her heels in, hoping to slow him down.

If Trevor's stomping had not scared the assailant, she probably would have been shot on the spot. But why? Who was this man?

Valerie stopped struggling for a moment. If she couldn't use force to get away, maybe reason would work. "Please, I'm an officer of the law. You'll go to jail for a long time."

The man spoke forcefully into her ear, his voice like a pounding drum. "With what I'm getting paid, lady, I can get away and never be found."

Panic coursed through her. Only the syndicate had that kind of money to hire someone to kill her. He kicked a door and dragged her through some kind of structure. It looked like they were on the ground floor of the apartment building under construction.

He grabbed the collar of her uniform at the back and pushed her forward. She fell on the concrete floor. He pulled the slide of his gun back and released a sinister chuckle. She rolled sideways and caught a glimpse of him, a colossus of a man with black wavy hair. His bulbous lips furled back from his mouth. He aimed the gun at her.

She took in a breath that felt like it was filled with jagged glass. Her stomach tightened into a hard ball as he lifted the gun. She couldn't outrun the bullet.

Then she heard it—the faint barking of

a dog. Her heart nearly burst with relief. Lexi was coming for her.

Panic filled the man's features as he lifted his head and turned, comprehending what the sound of the approaching dog meant.

Valerie used his moment of inattention to pull herself to her knees. Before she could get on her feet, he had run toward her, yanking her by the collar and pulling her up. The fabric choked her. She gasped for breath.

"Up those stairs," he commanded. He pushed her toward stairs that led to the second floor. She climbed, and he followed close on her heels.

The one thing she had in her favor was that this man did not want to be caught in the act of killing her. It had stopped him once. When she glanced behind her, he had the gun aimed at her. There was nowhere to go but up.

As she climbed, she could still hear Lexi's barking, but it had grown more distant. Had the dog been thrown off by some other smell? Trevor would only be able to guess at the right commands.

Oh, please, God, bring her to me.

When they stopped climbing, they came out on what must be the fourth or fifth floor, which consisted of a plywood floor and the metal framing of the outside walls. As he pushed her toward the edge of the structure, she could hear only the faint sounds of Lexi's searching.

"Back up more," the assailant ordered.

She stood on the edge of the floor. He'd shoot her, and she'd fall off the edge. If the bullet didn't kill her, the fall would. He lifted his gun and took aim. The trigger clicked. She closed her eyes and said goodbye to the life she had loved.

Lexi had taken the stairs to the second floor and then bolted up the ladder that led to the third without hesitation. Her ears were drawn back on her head as she focused only on moving ahead. As they reached the third floor, a popping sound slammed against Trevor's eardrum. Fear sliced through him. He tilted his head. A gunshot.

Dear God, don't let us be too late.

Lexi stopped and raised her head, letting out two quick barks. And then she ran for the ladder that led to the fourth floor. Helpless to do anything else, he followed the dog.

As they climbed, the sound of creaking metal surrounded them. Something crashed into something else on the outside of the building. Lexi came out on the fourth floor, which was empty except for some power tools and stacks of wood.

He heard another crashing noise and ran to the edge of the open floor. A large man with dark hair skirted around a work trailer and disappeared. Trevor's heart seized. Had that man shot Valerie and then run off?

Lexi ran the length of the floor with her nose to the ground.

Trevor edged toward the perimeter of the open floor, fearing the worst. He braced himself for a vision of Valerie's prone body on the ground, crumpled and deformed by the fall and bleeding from the bullet. When he peered over the edge, he saw only the construction materials and a work truck.

Lexi came to the edge of the floor opposite him, her bark insistent. She twirled in circles and barked again.

Trevor ran to where the dog kept returning. Lexi sat back on her haunches, barked and then got up, pacing. He peered over the edge. At first, he saw nothing. Lexi kept going to the edge of the floor, whining and looking up at Trevor. When he peered over the edge again, some of the scaffolding looked like it had given way and hung at a slant.

Lexi leaned over the edge and barked. Wild horses weren't going to drag her away from that spot. The dog knew something.

He looked again. "Valerie?"

Dare he hope?

No response came.

And then he saw it. Beneath the scaffolding that was at a slant, a hand. Trevor leapt over the side of the building and climbed down the scaffolding. When he looked up, Lexi was watching him. Her big ears flopped forward.

He reached out for the metal frame that held the plywood floor of the scaffold. The whole structure creaked and swayed. It wasn't as sturdy as it should be. He jumped to the scaffold that stood at a slant. Gripping the edge, he peered underneath it.

Valerie's hand was twisted in a piece of broken cable. Her head hung to one side.

He said her name again, but she didn't respond.

Aware that the scaffolding could give way, he inched toward her and reached out to grab her feet. He still saw no indication that she was alive. He shimmied to the edge of the plywood platform. The whole structure creaked. By leaning out and risking falling himself, he was able to wrap his hand around her waist and reach up to untwist the cable that had kept her from falling to the ground.

He gathered her into his arms. Her body was still warm. Blood stained the sleeve of her uniform. He brushed his hand over her face. She had hit her head on something, but she hadn't been shot there. He touched her stomach and her shoulders, no sign of a bullet hole or bleeding. His hand moved to her neck. Her pulse pushed back against his fingers.

Joy flooded through him, and he drew her close. She was alive. She was breathing.

He pressed his face against her cheek. "I thought I'd lost you." His throat tightened with emotion. He'd saved lives before because it was his job, but this was different. He had felt his heart open up to her in a way it never had before. He buried his face against her neck. "I didn't want to lose you."

In the distance, he heard the sound of sirens as backup pulled onto the street where they had received the false call for a domestic disturbance. It would be a matter of minutes before the cops figured out they were at the construction site.

Overcome with emotion he didn't understand, he held Valerie close and waited for her to regain consciousness. She had to be all right. She just had to be.

EIGHT

Valerie felt as though she were being pulled out of a deep pit, upward toward light and sound. Voices around her became more distinct.

She heard her mother. "You gave us quite a scare there, Junebug. Thank goodness there were no broken bones."

No matter how old she got, the sound of her mother's voice would always be a comfort.

Then she heard her father's gravelly voice, "She's a Salgado. She's made of indestructible iron, just like the rest of us."

Her eyes opened. She blinked. The images in front of her were blurry. Three indistinct faces surrounded her.

"There you are," her mother said again. A tender sound to her ears.

"Give her some space, people." That was her dad.

"Her pupils look normal." A third voice she didn't recognize.

She could feel people fussing around her, tucking blankets underneath her. The smell of bleach filled her nose. She was in a hospital bed. That third voice was probably a doctor.

Her mind struggled to put the memory back together about what had happened at the construction site. Knowing she was out of options, she had leapt off the building seconds before the large man had pulled the trigger, hoping he would think he had hit his target.

Her father stood by the bed. Her mother had pushed the wheelchair close. Her brother David and his wife, Mary, sat on chairs not too far away. Standing away from the others toward the back wall was Trevor. Her vision cleared. Trevor lifted his chin to indicate he saw her. There was a brightness in his eyes she hadn't seen before.

Then she remembered being held so tightly and someone crying over her. His voice had been a mixture of joy and anguish. She glanced again at Trevor, whose gaze was downcast. Was that really a memory or was her mind filling in blank spaces?

"Boy that dog was something else, wasn't she?" Her father turned slightly to address Trevor.

While she had been absorbing her surroundings, a conversation that she hadn't totally been aware of had been going on. The doctor had left the room.

Her mother leaned close to her and patted her hand. "We thought that dog wasn't going to let the doctor have a look at you."

"They had to call one of the trainers from the center to come over and get her," said her father. "Trevor said Lexi insisted on riding in the ambulance. Nothing anyone did or said would change her mind."

She'd come to in the ambulance only for a few moments. Lexi had licked her hand, and Trevor had hovered over her.

He had brushed her forehead with a touch so gentle for someone who was so strong. The concern for her etched in his features burned into her memory.

From the back wall where he stood, Trevor cleared his throat. "Lexi really proved herself out there today. She is completely devoted to Valerie. I don't think there is anything that dog wouldn't do for her."

Valerie settled back on her pillow. All the weeks of training she and Lexi had gone through had paid off. But it was more than the training that bonded them. She loved that dog and Lexi loved her.

Her mother rolled back from the bed. "I suppose we better let you get some rest. The doctor wanted to keep you overnight."

"Overnight." Valerie sat up. "Who is going to take care of Bethany?"

"Relax, honey, your friend Lucy said she could take her for the night. She'll bring her by first thing in the morning when you check out. It's all been taken care of."

Pain sliced through her arm. She must have scraped it in the fall, and her head hurt. Uneasiness stirred inside her. She wanted to be home with Lexi and Bethany. They were a family. They needed to be together.

Her family filed out with Trevor being the last to leave.

Tears warmed the corners of her eyes. The day had been too long and too hard. She missed Bethany. Her arms felt empty.

Trevor returned a few minutes later. "I just called the station. There'll be a night duty officer coming by in a few hours for protection. I can stay with you until he gets here."

She turned her head away and nodded. Reality hit her like a semi truck. The syndicate's desire to kill her had not gone away. If anything, what had happened today revealed how far they would go to kill her.

Trevor leaned over the bed. "You okay?"

She swiped at her eyes. "I'm missing Bethany. I know Lucy will take good care of her, but I'd feel better if I could be with her."

He studied her for a moment. "Do you want me to see if I can get you something to eat?"

She wiped another tear off her cheek. Her distress was probably too much for him to deal with, so he was focusing on doing things for her. "Just a drink of water would be nice."

He poured the water and held the cup, tilting the straw toward her mouth. She wasn't that injured, she could hold the cup herself, but he seemed to like helping her in that way. Absently, she draped her fingers over his beefy hand.

He sucked in a breath of air, and his eyes widened. She searched the depth of his dark brown eyes as heat spread over her skin. He looked away. Did he really not want her to see what was in those eyes? It had taken courage for him to share the darkness of his childhood. Maybe he was still afraid she would reject him over it.

She could not imagine what kind of a home he had known if it had ended with his father killing his mother.

The sound of her swallowing augmented in the silence between them. She finished drinking, and squeezed his fingers, hoping to communicate her acceptance of him.

Your secrets are safe with me, Trevor.

He pulled away and placed the plastic cup on the tray at the end of her bed. Then he sat down in a chair. "So that had to have been the Serpent who sent that guy to kill you. The whole thing was a setup."

Valerie pulled the covers up to her neck and shuddered. She didn't want to revisit the attack and could only manage a nod. How far did the syndicate's arms reach in this town, anyway?

Even as the fear returned over her own life being in jeopardy, resolve as hard as steel formed inside her. Her part in ending the control the syndicate had over Sagebrush was with identifying the Serpent and seeing that she was put in jail. Once she was back out on patrol, she could garner information that would lead to the downfall of the syndicate.

Trevor shifted in his chair. "I was thinking if Murke couldn't get a gun from his sister, he'll try to get one some other way."

Valerie nodded, grateful the subject had changed. "People I've arrested have dropped names about where they got the guns they used in crimes. We might be able to track some of these people down. With his record, Murke's not going to be able to get a gun legally."

He patted her shoulder. "We'll get started on it tomorrow." His voice filled with tenderness. "You've been through a lot. Why don't you get some sleep?"

She liked the way he used the word *we*. They were a team. Desire to catch Murke almost overshadowed her need for recovery. "You're probably right." She turned her head and closed her eyes. At first, her awareness of Trevor in the room made it hard to fall asleep, despite how exhausted she was. Gradually, the heaviness of unconsciousness invaded her mind like a fog. She drifted off.

She awoke once in the night. Trevor had propped a laptop up on a heater and was typing. He glanced in her direction when she stirred. His vigilance made her feel safe, but when was he going to sleep? He had been through almost as much as she had. She fell back asleep.

When she opened her eyes a second time, Trevor was gone. She stared at the empty chair for a moment as her heart filled with longing. The night officer must be stationed outside her door.

She stayed awake, listening to the sound of footsteps, the wheels of gurneys turning and faint conversations. She lay with her eyes open in the dark room. A chill crept beneath her skin. Though she told herself it was only the nighttime and the quiet of the room that was scaring her, she couldn't let go of her fear that one of the

Serpent's henchmen would burst through the door or break the window at any moment. Her sleep was fitful until morning sun streamed through the crack between the curtains.

Trevor met Slade McNeal at the end of the long hallway that led to Valerie's hospital room. The look on Slade's face was grim. A sudden dread gripped Trevor that something had happened to Valerie in the night.

Even though he knew Valerie didn't go on shift until later in the afternoon, he'd been anxious to check on her. He'd slept only a few hours at his hotel before worry over her safety had gotten him out of bed.

Though concern pressed on him, he kept his voice level and managed a smile. "McNeal, you coming to check on Valerie?"

"I was hoping to talk to her, but maybe she'd take the news a little better if it came from you." The captain placed his hands on his hips.

Trevor shook his head, not understanding where McNeal was leading.

"In light of what happened yesterday, I'm going to ask Valerie to take a couple of sick days until I can think things through. Both you and Lexi were with her, and the syndicate still found a way to get at her." The worry lines in McNeal's forehead became more pronounced. "I just don't know if she can do her job safely."

Though he didn't disagree with the decision, he doubted Valerie would be happy about it. "She wants to catch the members of the syndicate as much as you do. She's been a big help in chasing down Murke, but I understand your reasoning."

They walked together down the hall toward Valerie's room. "I hate doing it to her, but I can't put a good officer at risk. I'll see that she has protection while she's at home."

"I can stay with her this morning. We're trying to track down some of the guys that might sell Murke a gun under the table. We know from his half sister that he is trying to acquire one."

McNeal nodded. "Making some phone calls would be fine. It gives me some time to speak to the chief and move the duty roster around so we can provide her with more protection at her home."

As they made their way toward Valerie's hospital room, he saw Lucy enter, carrying Bethany in one hand and a car seat in the other.

Trevor had that sinking feeling that no matter how McNeal's decision was presented, Valerie wasn't going to take it well.

"There she is. There's my girl." Valerie thought her heart would burst into a thousand pieces when Lucy carried Bethany into the hospital room.

Bethany kicked her legs and reached out for Valerie, who was dressed and past ready to leave the hospital. The light blue floral dress with a ruffle offset Bethany's eyes. Lucy had placed a sunhat on Bethany's blond head. Valerie pulled her close and Bethany snuggled against her.

"She's a busy little thing." Lucy set the diaper bag down. "She kept me on my toes."

"Thanks, Lucy, for watching her," Valerie said.

"It was no trouble. I wish we could do more. You know that." Lucy pulled a teething ring out of the diaper bag. "She was fussy last night. I'm not sure what is up with that. She might have some teeth coming in."

Valerie looked into Bethany's blue eyes while she sucked on her teething ring and clutched her pink bunny. "She's still adjusting…to things. It's hard for her to sleep at night."

Lucy said her goodbyes, hugged Bethany and Valerie and left. Bethany wandered around the room while Valerie gathered her things. The shiny black buckle shoes made her little feet look so small.

Bethany pointed at the bed and said, "Ahh?" Her word for what is it?

"Bed. That's a bed, sweetie." Valerie held her hand out to her. "Come on, let's go." Bethany's hand slipped into hers. Valerie took smaller steps so Bethany could keep up with her. In the hallway, she was surprised to see Trevor and McNeal.

As she looked over at Trevor, the seriousness in his eyes gave her pause. Was he bringing bad news?

She swept Bethany into her arms. "I didn't expect to see you both here. I'm not on shift until later."

Trevor offered her a quick smile. "I thought I would keep you company."

She glanced from McNeal to Trevor. "What's going on?"

McNeal rubbed his temple. "I want you to take a few days off."

Valerie held Bethany a little tighter. "Why? I'm ready to go back to work. I feel fine…I just got a few bruises and scrapes." She couldn't do her part in taking down the syndicate if she was sitting at home.

"In light of what happened yesterday…" Trevor's gaze darted from McNeal to Valerie. "He seems to think you might be in too much danger on the streets."

"Are you thinking I need to be on desk duty for a while?" She loved doing patrol with Lexi. Sitting at a desk would drive her insane, but at least she would still in some way be helping take down the syndicate.

McNeal shook his head. "I don't know. I just know it's not safe for you to be out on patrol."

Valerie gazed at Trevor for a moment. It annoyed her that he wasn't protesting McNeal's decision—especially since he of all people knew she could handle herself.

Valerie clenched her teeth. So she wasn't even going to get desk duty. What if McNeal decided she couldn't do her job at all? A couple of days could turn into weeks. She knew they only wanted to keep her safe, but being on patrol was like breathing to her. "I could have died out there yesterday, and I didn't."

"You made incredibly smart choices." Trevor's voice tinged with admiration. "I just don't think the police department fathomed the power and the resources the syndicate would utilize to get at you."

Frustration rose to the surface. "If only I could remember who this woman was… where I've seen her before."

McNeal gripped her forearm. "I know this is not what you wanted to hear, but I have to keep my officers safe." He turned and headed down the long hallway.

Valerie's throat went tight as she watched her captain disappear around a corner. Couldn't he see that she only wanted to do her job?

"McNeal said take the day off, so do as he says and enjoy yourself. I'll keep you company." Trevor's voice held a tone of false cheerfulness. He was trying to make her feel better, but why hadn't he stood up for her more?

"I guess I have no choice." Bethany rested her head against Valerie's neck as if to comfort her. "I'm going to call Slade later so he can clarify whether this is a few days or until the Serpent is in custody." The prospect of being a prisoner in her home or having to restrict her movements for months frustrated her.

They stepped out into the sunlight of early morning, and Trevor directed her to his car. She placed the car seat Lucy had brought in the backseat.

Once they were settled in, Trevor turned to her. "So what's the plan?"

"We need to go get Lexi. I was planning on taking her and Bethany to the park this morning, anyway…so we might as well do that."

"All right then, let's go." Trevor's effort at trying to sound positive was commendable, but none of it made McNeal's decision sting any less.

How long would this go on? If only she could remember the woman's face more clearly. She had sat down with a police artist twice and attempted to recall the details in the face she'd seen for a split second, but always the image was blurry. They looked through police photographs of women who had a record. Nothing clicked.

Trevor started his car. "Where am I going?"

"Same park as where the dog had her pups yesterday." Valerie laced her hands together and tried to let go of the bad news that had started her day. She looked out the window. It was a beautiful sunny day. The sound of Bethany babbling in the backseat lifted her spirits. She needed to focus on what was right in her life.

After getting Lexi from the training facility, Trevor pulled into a lot of the park that faced a duck pond. "This all right?"

She rolled the window down, enjoying the warmth of the morning sun. Maybe by the end of the day McNeal would change his mind. "Let's go have some fun."

Trevor carried the diaper bag while Valerie lifted Bethany out of her car seat. She rubbed noses with the little girl, which caused a squeal of delight. Bethany offered her a smile, revealing a front row of pearl-white teeth. "How could anyone be sad around you, huh?"

Lexi followed dutifully behind as they found a park bench. Valerie pulled a flat beach ball out of Bethany's bag and blew it up. She rolled it toward Bethany who sat in the grass a few feet from the bench.

Valerie sat down on the grass beside Bethany, and the dog situated herself close by.

Trevor paced the length of the bench and then walked a half circle around them. Valerie rolled the ball to Bethany. Trevor stopped and stared at a grove of trees. His posture stiffened.

Valerie followed the line of his gaze. Her heartbeat kicked up a notch when she saw the man partly shielded by the trees looking in their direction.

NINE

Trevor zeroed in on the man in the wooded area. The stranger slipped deeper into the trees and disappeared. Why was he trying to conceal himself?

Still not willing to let his guard down, Trevor surveyed the park, making a note of every person within a hundred yards of them and watching the comings and goings in the parking lot. Behind the bench, a jogging trail ran along the upward slope of the hill. Though he could keep an eye on the people in front of them, someone could come up over the hill and close in on them without much warning.

An open park like this was precarious in terms of safety for Valerie. However, she'd had a traumatic day and a disappointing morning. He didn't want to add to her frustration by telling her she couldn't take her niece to the park.

Bethany lifted the beach ball and carried it toward Lexi. The dog nudged the ball with her nose, and Bethany clapped her hands in delight. The Rottweiler wagged her tail. Valerie remained close to Bethany, talking into her ear and pointing. She twisted her long red hair and held it in place before looking over at Trevor.

That open and honest gaze that she had was enough to make him weak in the knees. She was a beautiful woman. And once the Serpent was caught and this was all over, she would have a beautiful life, a little girl to care for and job she loved. He had seen the worst of humanity in his life and his work. Even as he felt his heart opening to her, he knew they were two very different people.

A car pulled into the lot, and a large man with black hair got out. Trevor moved a little closer to Valerie. Tension eased when the man opened the back door and two young boys tumbled out.

As he drew closer, the man only vaguely resembled the assailant from yesterday. The boys both placed sailboats in the pond. The man took a bench on the opposite side of the pond.

Valerie studied the woods where he had seen the man. Her mouth twitched, and a look of sadness clouded her features for only a moment before she managed a smile. Her efforts at not giving in to despair were deliberate.

Bethany had just rolled the ball down the hill toward the pond when Trevor noticed the man sitting on a bench on their side of the pond. The same man he had seen hiding in the trees. Valerie and Bethany walked toward the pond with Lexi trailing behind. The ball slipped into the water.

Trevor hurried down the hill toward Valerie, training his glance toward the man without turning his head. The man wore a jacket that was too heavy for the warm weather and could easily conceal a gun.

Bethany and Valerie made an utterance of disappointment as the ball rolled into the pond. Valerie commanded Lexi to get the ball. Without hesitation, the dog jumped in the water, but only managed to push the ball toward the center of the pond.

The man in the coat sat on the bench above them. Trevor glanced up at him. The man's gaze followed Valerie as she moved closer to the water.

Lexi got out of the water on the side of the pond, some distance from Valerie and Bethany. The two boys with sailboats cheered and clapped, encouraging the ball to float completely across the water.

Trevor swooped down the hill. "Why don't we go for a walk?" He pulled Valerie up by the elbow.

"But we need to get the ball." She opened her mouth to protest more and then noticed the man on the bench rising to his feet. "Oh." Her voice filled with fear.

She gathered up Bethany. Trevor fell in step behind her, and Lexi took up the rear. When he looked at the bench again, the man was gone. He wouldn't try to take a shot at them as long as they were in the open and around people, unless he could shield himself from view.

Trevor placed a protective hand on the middle of Valerie's back, a move that made Lexi grunt in protest.

Trevor looked at Lexi and shook his head.

We're both trying to do the same job, girl.

"She doesn't like it when you touch me." Valerie kept her voice upbeat, but her gaze darted around at her surroundings.

There were a dozen trees the stranger could hide behind.

Trevor pointed to a gazebo by an ice-cream stand. "Let's go over there." The gazebo was in a flat, open area. He would have a full three-sixty view of the park.

As she sat down in the gazebo, Valerie said, "Maybe we should just go home." She kept her voice sing-songy for Bethany's sake, but he picked up on the undercurrent of tension.

Trevor took a seat opposite them. He wanted her to have at least a few hours where the threat wasn't foremost in her mind. Couldn't he at least give her that? "We'll be fine here. That man could have just been out for a walk."

Valerie let out a heavy sigh. Bethany wiggled out of her arms and sat on the wooden floor of the gazebo. She continued to talk to the child in a positive tone, but Trevor saw the pensiveness in her eyes.

"Come on, I'll buy you two some ice cream. Isn't that what people do in parks?"

"It's kind of early in the day, but sure," Valerie shrugged. "Since Bethany can't eat a whole cone, just ask for a spoon and I'll give her bites of mine."

Trevor stepped out of the gazebo and walked a few feet to the ice-cream stand. "Can I get two vanilla cones?"

"Coming right up." The ice cream vendor's white apron covered his rotund belly. His bald spot glistened in the morning sun.

Trevor turned to check on Valerie, who had gotten down on her knees to point things out to Bethany as she took in her surroundings. Lexi stood guard outside the gazebo.

The man handed Trevor an ice-cream cone with a generous scoop. "That's a nice family you got there."

Was that how they looked to the outside world? Just a family enjoying a morning in the park. No one else could see the level of fear Valerie lived with every moment. "Thank you," Trevor said as he took the second cone from him.

Trevor resumed his spot on the bench in the gazebo and watched Valerie give

Bethany spoons full of ice cream while the little girl held on to Valerie's leg and bounced. Her mouth opened bird-like every time Valerie tried to get a bite of ice cream for herself.

"She's getting more of that than you are."

"That's usually how it works." Valerie wiped Bethany's ice-cream-stained face with a paper napkin.

A chuckle escaped his throat. He couldn't help it—watching Bethany made him smile. Valerie relaxed, too. She laughed as Bethany tried to grab the spoon to feed herself.

Trevor's cell phone rang. "Agent Lewis."

The voice that came across the line had a slow Texas drawl. "This is Detective Jackson Worth. I think I may have a sighting on your fugitive."

Trevor sat up a little straighter. "Really?"

"A man matching Derek Murke's description just checked in to the Rainbow

Motel—it's a fleabag not too far from the industrial district."

Trevor's voice betrayed his excitement. "How did you find out?"

"I kind of put a bug in the ear of a couple of people in that area I know I can trust. One of them saw a man matching his description going into the hotel."

"How long ago did he check in?"

"I got the call less than an hour ago," Jackson said.

"Thanks, I'll look into it." Trevor slammed his phone shut. The elation he felt over a new lead faded when he saw the drawn look on Valerie's face.

"So sounds like you may have found Murke." She offered him a faint smile, but her eyes never brightened. "That's good news."

"I'll take you and Bethany home." As anxious as he was to see if the lead checked out, he understood her frustration at being put out of commission. He'd never been very good at sitting still and doing nothing if he knew he could put a criminal in jail. She was probably the same way.

She nodded and bit her lower lip. "I guess I'll just have to enjoy my day off." She sounded like she was trying to convince herself.

They walked back across the park to his car. He drove her back to her place, calling to make sure a police officer would be posted outside her house as soon as possible.

The officer had just pulled into place when he brought his car to the curb.

Trevor escorted Valerie and Bethany to her house, then searched both floors and walked around to the fenced backyard before he was satisfied that no one was lying in wait for her.

As he drove away, Valerie stood at the window.

Unable to reach McNeal by phone, Valerie spent the afternoon cleaning her already clean kitchen. McNeal owed her an answer as to how long her exile would go on. What she feared most was that he would ask her to take a permanent leave of absence until the Serpent was behind bars.

By late afternoon, she had worked off some of her frustration. Fatigue set in as she lay Bethany down for a nap. The physical trauma of yesterday's confrontation was catching up with her.

Before lying down to rest, she checked to see the officer parked outside. The afternoon sky had darkened with the promise of rain. Always a welcome event in southwest Texas.

Bethany lay in her bed on her tummy. Her cheeks rosy and her downy hair sticking out at all angles. She had seemed fussier than usual before her nap. Valerie stroked the toddler's back and then lay down herself to sleep.

She awoke hours later to the sound of Bethany's crying. Wind rattled the glass panes, and the sky had grown dark.

Bethany's cry sounded different than her usual I'm-awake-please-hold-me cry.

Valerie sat up and threw back the covers. Bethany wasn't standing up in her crib. Instead, she continued to lie on her tummy rubbing her face against the blankets.

Lexi whined from the door where she'd been standing watch.

When she gathered the toddler into her arms, the heat of the little body stunned her. Her cheeks were even redder and her forehead was hot. Valerie tried to soothe the little girl.

"You got some teeth coming in? Is that what's going on?" When she opened Bethany's mouth, the gums didn't look swollen. Maybe it was something more serious.

Valerie stared at the ceiling as she fought against the onslaught of anxious thoughts. Bethany had seemed fine this afternoon. But Lucy had said she was fussy the night before. Maybe it hadn't just been about being away from familiar surroundings.

Bethany rested her chin on Valerie's

shoulder and continued to fuss and cry, wiggling and writhing in Valerie's arms. Her little body stiffening in pain. "You poor thing."

Worry spread through her as she made her way downstairs to the kitchen to find the children's fever reducer. Bethany cried louder when Valerie put her in the playpen, so she could root through the drawer where she kept baby medicine, ointments and bandages.

When she opened the bottle of fever reducer, it was empty. How could she have been so forgetful to not pick up more? What kind of mom was she to let her baby be in pain like this?

Bethany's crying became more intense. She touched Bethany's hot cheek and then put the thermometer in her ear. She read the digital numbers. 101. Not good.

She needed to get Bethany's fever down so she would sleep. She paced the floor and then picked up the phone and dialed Mrs. Witherspoon's number. The phone rang five times before the answering machine came on. Lucy wasn't answering her phone, either.

She grabbed the empty medicine bottle, slipped into her coat and raced outside, tapping on the window of the officer on duty.

"I need you to do something for me. My little girl is sick. I need to get her some more of this." She showed him the bottle.

"Ma'am, I'm not supposed to leave my post."

"Please, it will take you twenty minutes at the most. There's an all-night drugstore ten blocks away. It would be more dangerous if I went out myself, and I don't want to take my little girl out in this rain."

The officer stared at the bottle of medicine.

"Please, for my little girl. She'll have a miserable night if I don't break her fever."

He nodded. "Okay, but don't tell my supervisor I did this."

She watched his two red taillights distorted by the rain as he drove away, and then ran back inside where Bethany continued to cry. Lexi paced and whined by Bethany's playpen. The dog licked Bethany's fingers, something she had never done before. Lexi's concern for Bethany indicated that she was bonding to the little girl.

Valerie stroked the Rottweiler's head and ears. "I know you want to make it better, don't you?"

She swept Bethany up and walked back and forth the length of the kitchen floor while bouncing Bethany and singing to her. The little girl stiffened in her arms and tugged at her ear. Her cheeks flushed a deep red from the fever.

Valerie felt like her heart had tied itself into knots. The worst thing in the world was seeing your child in pain. Bethany stopped wailing for a moment and stared up at Valerie with her wide blue eyes.

She pressed her face against Bethany's hot cheek and could almost feel the child's pain.

My baby. My sweet baby.

Bethany took in a shaky breath and resumed her crying. Her little body was rigid from pain. The doctor wouldn't be open at this hour, but if she could get the fever down, she could have a restful night. In the morning, if the fever came back, she'd have to see the pediatrician.

Valerie walked a circle through the living room and kitchen with Lexi following her. When twenty minutes passed and the officer hadn't returned, she peeked out the window. A car she didn't recognize was parked across the street. An icy chill crept over her skin. Was her fear real or imagined? Someone in the neighborhood could just have a visitor.

She picked her cell phone up off the kitchen counter where she had left it. Calling the department would get the officer in trouble. It wouldn't look good to McNeal, either, for her being put back on duty. Maybe she hadn't made the best choice in sending the officer to the pharmacy, but concern for Bethany took priority over everything else.

She ran her fingers over the control

panel of the phone. Maybe she could call Trevor. She dismissed the thought. He was working surveillance trying to track down Murke. It would be selfish to call him away from his job.

Maybe he had even caught Murke by now. Sadness and frustration over not being able to be a part of such a coup was like a knife to her heart.

Bethany screamed in her ear and then rubbed her face against Valerie's shoulders.

Valerie prayed for her fever to go away.

Where was the police officer? Her mind grasped for an explanation. Maybe he hadn't been able to find the fever reducer and had gone to look at a different store. Valerie moved one more time to the window where the strange car was still parked.

She picked up the phone again. Maybe she should call Trevor now?

Trevor had watched the entrance of the Rainbow Motel all day and into the evening with no sign of Murke. Showing Murke's picture to the desk clerk meant that the fugitive might be tipped off. He didn't want to risk it.

The motel was situated in a less than desirable part of town that featured a lot of bars and greasy-spoon restaurants and secondhand stores. Sitting here watching the door of the motel was starting to feel like a waste of time. Maybe the guy who had checked in only looked like Murke. However, he wasn't ready to let go just yet. Maybe Murke had spent time in some of the businesses around here. Someone might recognize his picture.

After alerting the other surveillance unit of what he was doing, Trevor pushed open his car door, turned up the collar of his coat against the rain and walked up the sidewalk. He peered into a window of one of the restaurants. Most of the customers ate alone at the counter. One table had a mother and father sitting with their two children. He watched for a moment as the mother scooped up applesauce and fed it to a baby who wasn't much younger than Bethany. Funny how his thoughts went back to the little girl.

He'd lingered at the window long enough for people to start to look at him. Best to go inside and see if he could spot Murke. As he opened the door to the restaurant, a cacophony of noises assaulted him, people talking, dishes clattering, waitresses yelling at cooks.

Several people craned their necks in his direction as he stepped inside. The place was dimly lit, making it hard to see the faces of the people in the booths. He found a chair at the counter and ordered a soda. He walked the length of the room, studying each face without staring. He stepped into the men's room where the walls muffled the noises, waited a moment and then stepped back outside. He performed the same discreet survey of faces on his way back.

The waitress had left his soda by his place at the counter. He drank slowly, swung around on his stool and did one more survey of the restaurant.

"Can I get you anything else, honey?" With her steel-gray hair and heavily lidded eyes, the waitress was probably someone's grandmother.

"No, thank you." Trevor put his empty glass back on the counter. He pulled the photo of Murke out of his chest pocket. "Can you do one thing for me? Can you tell me if this man has ever come in here to eat?"

The waitress put his bill on the counter, glanced at the photograph and shook her head. "He sure looks like a mean one, but I ain't seen him around here."

Understatement of the century. He gathered up the photograph. Maybe the Rainbow Motel was a dead end, after all.

Trevor put payment for the soda and a tip on the counter, then walked toward the door.

When he stepped outside, light rain sprinkled down on him. Across the street, teenagers had set up a makeshift game of soccer in an empty lot. He watched them kick the ball through the mud, slapping each other on the back and offering verbal jabs as they raced across their small field.

The rain distorted the lights from the streetlamps and the whole scene had a surreal quality to it. He couldn't help but think that if Valerie were with him, she would strike up a conversation with the teens if she didn't know them already. Yes, his thoughts always seemed to circle back to her, too.

He turned and headed back toward the hotel. He'd give surveillance one more hour. He had just opened his car door when his phone rang.

Valerie's phone number came up on the screen. "Hello?"

"Trevor." The single word carried a note of desperation.

"Valerie, what is it?" He could hear Bethany crying in the background. His heart lurched. "What's going on?"

"I sent the officer away to get some fever reducer for Bethany. It's been forty minutes. He hasn't come back. There's this car outside that concerns me. I know you are working, but I didn't know who else to call."

"I'll be right over." He hung up and ran the half block to his car. After informing the other surveillance team that he was leaving, he shifted into gear and sped toward Valerie's house, praying that nothing bad happened to her before he got there.

TEN

Lexi's scratching at the sliding glass door was insistent.

"You have to go, don't you?" Valerie had been so preoccupied with Bethany, she'd forgotten about Lexi. Bethany had settled into a fitful sleep in her playpen, waking and crying every ten minutes.

Valerie slid open the door. The steady fall of rain greeted her ears. Lexi slipped past her. The dog's dark fur disappeared against the blackness of the night as she ran to the edge of the yard. Only the tinkling of dog tags indicated where she was. "Come on, Lex. Hurry it up."

Valerie took in a breath of rain-freshened air. Though worry still plagued her over Bethany and over the officer's delay in returning, she had breathed a sigh of relief when she heard Trevor's voice over the phone. He was on his way.

Inside the house, Bethany wailed. Valerie slid the glass door shut and ran to get her. Lexi let out two quick barks. She gathered Bethany in her arms, walking and swaying with her to quiet her. She worked her way back to the sliding glass door, opened it and called for Lexi. All she could hear was the pattering of the rain.

"Lexi?" Panic coursed through her. "Lexi!" she shouted. Lexi had never run away before. Bethany wiggled in her arms. She couldn't stand out in the rain with the baby, and she couldn't leave Bethany alone to look for Lexi.

She tried one more time calling for Lexi as a sense of foreboding overtook her. Aware suddenly of how vulnerable she was, she closed the door and latched it. The police officer was gone. Lexi was gone. Valerie could feel the walls closing in on her as Bethany's cries echoed in her ears. She raced upstairs and placed Bethany in her crib.

She opened the window that faced the backyard to see if she could see anything. The porch light illuminated only a small area close to the house. The rest of the yard was still dark. No sign of Lexi anywhere. Her breath caught as she shook her head in disbelief. This couldn't be happening. Someone had taken her dog…or worse.

This had gone too far. It was time to alert the police. She needed to go downstairs, get her cell phone and call the station.

Bethany stood up in her crib, shaking the railing and crying.

"I know, baby. I know you're hurting." She gathered Bethany into her arms.

Bethany wailed, jerking her head back. Valerie patted and rubbed her back. Bethany pressed close to her shoulder, her cry reduced to a whimper.

Silence enveloped them, as Valerie's

mind filled with anxiety over what had happened to Lexi.

Downstairs, a window shattered.

Trevor struggled to stay under the speed limit as he got closer to Valerie's house. He understood her desperation, but it was foolhardy to send the protective officer away. Why hadn't she just called him in the first place?

As he neared a stretch of road that led to her subdivision, flashing police lights caused a knot of tension to form at the base of his neck. He pulled his car over. A police car had been run off the road, and an ambulance had been called to the scene. He recognized one of the policemen talking to a woman, who had probably witnessed the accident. Trevor approached him.

"What happened here?"

"As you can see…someone ran one of our own off the road." The officer pointed to the police car angled into the ditch with a crushed front end and bent back bumper. "Knocked him up pretty good, too. He lost consciousness."

Trevor didn't know the name of the policeman assigned to watch Valerie, but he suspected it was the officer being loaded into the ambulance. Somebody didn't want that cop to make it back to Valerie's house. "Do they know what the cause of the accident was?"

"It looked to me like a black car hit the patrol car on purpose," said the witness. The woman fanned herself with her hand and shook her head. "And then he just drove off."

Trevor didn't wait around for further explanation. He jumped in his car and sped up the street to Valerie's house. He wrestled with his fear as he gripped the steering wheel. If anything happened to her, he didn't know if he could forgive himself. He should have stayed with her and let someone else run the surveillance on Murke.

He braked forcefully and jumped out of the car. When he knocked on the door, there was no answer. Anxiety coiled around his chest, making it hard to breathe. He knocked again, this time harder. When he tried the door, it was locked.

He ran around to the side of the house, but paused when he noticed a main-floor window that had been shattered. Had the storm done that? He reached inside, undid the latch and crawled through the window. He thought to call out Valerie's name, but caught himself. Something about the room felt off.

The main-floor area was eerily quiet. Valerie's phone rested on the counter-top in the kitchen. A bottle was on the kitchen table. Lexi hadn't come out to bark at him. Then he saw the rock on the carpet not far from the broken window.

With his heart pounding against his rib cage, he drew his gun and moved slowly up the stairs. The bedroom was empty. One of Bethany's blankets lay on the floor in a haphazard way in sharp contrast to the otherwise tidy room. His anxiety grew when he pushed open the closet door, but found nothing.

When he stepped back into the hallway, Valerie was pointing her gun at him. She let out a breath as her hand went limp.

"Why didn't you call out for me? I thought you were the intruder." Her voice was shaking from the adrenaline rush.

Even though his heart was still racing from having had a gun pointed at him, a sense of joy spread through him. Valerie was okay. "I saw signs of a break-in. I wanted to have the element of surprise on my side if the intruder was still around."

Bethany's cry came from what must be an upstairs bathroom.

Valerie set her gun on the hallway table and went into the bathroom. She returned a moment later, holding Bethany. The little girl's cheeks were red, and she sucked on her fingers. The distraught look on Valerie's face intensified as she tried to comfort the fussing baby.

Valerie talked at a rapid pace, growing more and more distraught. "I heard a window break when I was upstairs with Bethany."

"Someone did break a window, but it was still latched. Something scared them away."

Valerie didn't seem to be able to process that the intruder had been foiled. The panic-stricken look on her face never wavered. "I couldn't get to my phone. I left it downstairs. I grabbed my gun and hid in the bathroom." Her voice faltered. "I didn't know what else to do. Oh, Trevor, Lexi is gone."

Bethany stopped crying and rubbed her face against Valerie.

Trevor wanted to alleviate Valerie's distress—not add to it—but it looked like some careful planning had gone into the attack. It had probably involved several people if they had been able to take Lexi and run the police officer off the road. "How long ago did you hear the window break?"

"Maybe five minutes before I heard you in the hall."

So it had been his arrival that had scared the would-be intruders away. "I'll help you look for Lexi. We'll get some more protection here for you."

Bethany took her fingers out of her mouth and cried.

"Please, the first thing we need to do is get Bethany some fever reducer from the drugstore up the street."

Such a small thing in the gamut of everything that had happened in the last hour. "Sure, I can take you."

"I'll call the station. Maybe they can bring a K-9 tracking unit out here to look for Lexi. I have a feeling someone has hurt her or taken her." Valerie's agitation showed in her wavering voice and the deep crevice between her eyebrows.

He'd do anything to ease her worry, but he didn't know what to say. "We'll find her." He tried to sound reassuring, but what if the Serpent had done something horrible to Lexi and tossed her out on the road somewhere? Just the thought of it chilled him to the bone.

Valerie looked up at him, her eyes filled with pain. "I hope so."

Bethany quieted for a moment, resting her head against Valerie's neck. Trevor reached up and touched the toddler's tear-stained cheek. "We'll do all we can to find her," he said.

Valerie's lips parted slightly, and she managed a nod. He found himself leaning toward her, wanting to kiss her, to comfort her and hold her. Would his love be enough to calm her? In an instant, she blinked and looked away.

"I can grab my coat and phone downstairs." She swept past him. Her arm brushed over his. "I'll call the station before we go."

He followed behind her. Bethany looked over Valerie's shoulder, studying him.

As they drove to the drugstore, Bethany continued to cry. Valerie turned toward him. "Can you just go inside and get it? Bethany is so fussy. I'll wait out here with her."

Trevor glanced around at the parking

lot. The syndicate was pulling out all the stops to get at Valerie tonight. He wasn't about to leave her alone for even a few minutes. "You better come with me. I have no idea what I'm supposed to get. What if I get the wrong thing?"

Valerie scanned the area around her as well and let out a heavy breath. "I suppose you're right."

He didn't need to mention the syndicate by name for her to know that was what he was thinking about.

Valerie pushed open the door and got Bethany out of the backseat. The little girl quieted again when Valerie lifted her out of the car seat and placed a blanket over her.

The neon sign of the all-night drugstore had a warm, welcoming glow as did the lights inside the store, which seemed to cast a golden hue over everything. There were only a few other patrons in the store at this hour. An elderly couple waited by the pharmacy counter and a teenaged girl dressed all in black browsed through cosmetics. Neither seemed like a threat. All the same, he watched the door and the parking lot.

Valerie swayed and bounced with Bethany as they stood in front of the shelves of children's medicine.

"Which one do you want?" Trevor asked.

"I need to read the labels." She handed Bethany over to Trevor before he could protest.

Still obviously in pain, Bethany slammed her head against Trevor's chest, but didn't cry. Her little hand reached up and held on to his shirt collar. He could hear the sucking noises she made as she placed her fingers in her mouth. Her head was clammy from the fever, but her body was warm against his. Her chest moved in and out, pressing against his own.

Valerie picked up several bottles and read them front and back. "I don't remember which one Kathleen used to get…" When she looked at Trevor, her expression suddenly changed. The worry seemed to fall from her face and was replaced by a warmth that softened her features and made her even prettier. "You don't need to look so scared. You're doing just fine with her."

"I just…" He didn't want Bethany to break into a million pieces, but he couldn't tell Valerie that. It sounded ridiculous when he thought about it. "She seems so fragile."

"She's stays pretty calm when *you* hold her." Valerie stepped a little closer to him. "I think she likes you."

"She's just sick, is all," he said, dismissing the idea that anything he could do would comfort a child.

Valerie reached up and soothed Bethany's hair. "This is the quietest she's been all night."

Valerie's hand brushed the bottom of his chin. Heat rose up his face when he looked into the deep green of her eyes. Once again, he wondered what it would be like to kiss her. Right there in the aisle of the all-night drugstore, he was thinking about how soft and full her lips were.

What would it be like to pull her close and hold her? To breathe in the sweet smell she exuded.

The moment of reverie was broken by the sound of sirens on the street.

"That must be the units coming to help look for Lexi," Valerie said, her face contorted with worry.

"We should probably get back to the house so you can brief them on what you know." After picking out two different fever reducers, they raced out to the car and headed up the street.

Valerie took a deep breath to try to dispel some of the fear that was making her chest tight. Her house, with two police units parked outside, came into view. A new wave of tension caused her muscles to contract. What if Lexi was dead?

Bethany's low-level fussing in the backseat only added to her anxiety. She felt pulled in two directions and helpless. She couldn't leave Bethany to go look for Lexi.

"I suppose you will want to lend a hand with finding Lexi," Valerie said.

Of course he would. Trevor was the type who had to be part of the action, not doing something as mundane as taking care of a sick baby.

He studied her for a moment. "Looks like they have enough men on this. I'll stay with you until Bethany quiets down." His gaze flicked around the car and he added, "If you want me to."

"I'd like that," she murmured. Trevor was full of surprises. She hadn't realized how wearing it was to deal with a sick baby alone. His presence did seem to make the worry and anxiety more bearable. "I'll go tell them what I know, if you want to get Bethany out of her car seat."

She saw that flash of fear in his face again and couldn't help smiling. "It's easy to take her out. Just unclick the latch and lift her. Be careful not to hit her head on the door frame." How ironic to see this man, who could probably take down half a dozen criminals, single-handedly turn to a puddle of mush around a toddler.

The bloodhound Justice and his handler, Austin Black, from the K-9 Unit waited for her on her lawn. Justice's tracking skills were second to none. She approached Detective Black.

"I'm glad you could make it out here to help. The backyard was the last place I saw her." Her throat had gone tight from the surge of emotion over the loss of Lexi.

Compassion etched across Detective Black's face as he squeezed her elbow. "We'll find her."

"She wouldn't run away. Someone took her. I just know they did." She couldn't hide her desperation. Life without Lexi was unimaginable.

Austin looked toward the door of her house where Trevor had just stepped inside. "Looks like you got your hands full. We'll take care of this."

As she retreated toward the house with the sound of the baying bloodhound pressing on her ears, the feeling of being pulled in two directions intensified. She longed to be a part of the search. It would ease the angst if she could be doing something to find Lexi. But the thought of leaving Bethany tore her insides up.

When she stepped into her house, Bethany was crying. Trevor held on to her while she arched her back.

"What should I do?" The helplessness on his face was endearing.

"Sit down with her in the rocking chair. I'll get her medicine measured out." Every cry from Bethany was like a stab to Valerie's heart. She'd do anything for her not to be in pain. She'd take the pain on herself if she could. She measured the medicine out into a syringe and hurried into the living room.

"She doesn't like having the medicine. You're going to have to hold her so she can't turn her head away," Valerie said.

Trevor's eyes grew wide.

"She'll be all right. Just hold her chin with her mouth open. Then I can shoot this far enough down her throat so she won't spit it out."

Trevor's forehead wrinkled. "Are you sure about that?"

"Trevor, I've done this before. She needs this medicine."

Gingerly, he cupped his fingers around Bethany's chin.

Valerie soothed Bethany's hot cheek. "All right baby, open your mouth for me."

Bethany jerked her head to the side. Trevor pressed his hand flat against Bethany's cheek and pulled her mouth open with his thumb. Valerie shot the medicine toward the back of Bethany's throat before she had time to react.

Bethany's features pinched together in a look of utter betrayal.

"I'm so sorry, pumpkin." Valerie stroked her blond head.

Trevor sat back in the rocking chair. "Whew. Glad that's over." He continued to rock Bethany as her crying subsided.

Valerie returned the medicine to the kitchen cabinet. When she looked across the island into the living room, Bethany was gripping Trevor's finger while he pretended to try to pull away. Then he bent his head toward Bethany's and a look of pure delight filled Trevor's face as he elicited a smile from the sick little girl.

The moment passed quickly when he glanced up and saw Valerie. He frowned and bent his head self-consciously. He seemed almost embarrassed that she had caught him showing affection for Bethany.

After getting Bethany a bottle, Valerie collapsed on the love seat opposite the rocking chair. She was beyond exhausted.

"Do you want to take her?"

"You're fine. Let me catch my breath." She tilted her head and closed her eyes as the heaviness of fatigue settled in.

She rested for maybe fifteen minutes. When she opened her eyes, Bethany was taking the bottle while Trevor held her. Her eyelids flicked up and down and then closed altogether as she sucked on the bottle.

Trevor's stiff posture had softened a bit. He stared down at Bethany. What was he thinking right now? Did he care about Bethany or was she just an encumbrance to getting his job done? Why, then, had he offered to stay with them when he could have been part of the action combing the countryside for Lexi?

She wondered, too, what he had been thinking when he looked at her so intensely at the drugstore. He had leaned toward her as though to kiss her. She'd seen the smolder in his eyes and been pulled in by the magnetic force of his gaze. As the hours passed and they took turns rocking Bethany, the glow from the sunlight spread across the living room, giving everything a warm, golden quality. She wondered if maybe there could be something more between her and Trevor than a working relationship.

Trevor lifted his gaze toward her. That same look, filled with longing, colored his features and brought light to his eyes. Something had changed between them after their long night together with Bethany.

"Looks like you got her to sleep," Valerie murmured.

"I didn't think I would ever experience something like that." He looked down at the sleeping toddler. "Have a baby fall asleep in my arms."

She detected just a tiny hitch of emotion in his voice.

She heard baying and voices at her back door and got up to see what the noise was about. Her heart fluttered as she neared the sliding glass door. She opened it, half-expecting to see Lexi with her heavy jowls and dark eyes and her little bobbed tail vibrating in joy at seeing Valerie.

Detective Black stood outside, holding the leash while Justice sniffed the grass in vacuum-like fashion.

Valerie's hand went to her heart. "Did you find her?"

Austin Black shook his head, unable to hide his disappointment. "We lost the trail. I brought Justice back to see if we could pick it up again. I'm concerned that maybe at the point we lost the trail, Lexi was stashed in a car and taken somewhere."

Valerie took in a painful breath. What was the syndicate doing to poor Lexi?

Austin's voice filled with compassion. "I want to find her as bad as you do, Valerie. I know how much she means to you."

Valerie thanked Austin and returned to the living room with a heavy heart. Trevor, still holding Bethany, had drifted off to sleep. They looked so cute together. Both Trevor's and Bethany's head were angled to one side, their mouths slightly open…almost like they were father and daughter.

Valerie gathered the sleeping baby in her arms and trod upstairs to her room. She lay Bethany on her tummy, rubbed her back a few times and placed a blanket over her. Bethany stirred, rubbing her face against the sheet. Valerie braced for another bout of crying, but the baby quieted and grew still.

She tiptoed toward the door.

Trevor was standing in the hallway waiting. With his broad shoulders and firm jawline, he was still an imposing figure. But she felt as though she had seen a softer, more vulnerable side to him.

"She still sleeping?"

Nodding, Valerie turned and eased the door shut.

When she pivoted, Trevor was standing even closer to her. He gathered her in his arms, drawing her close and pressing his lips on top of hers.

She responded to his kiss. A tingly sensation, like warm honey moving through her veins, overtook her. Her hand rested on the hard muscle of his chest. He backed her up to a wall and deepened his kiss.

With his face still close to hers, he pulled her away from the wall and encircled her with his strong arms. He held her close. His kiss had left her breathless and wobbly in the knees. Trevor didn't seem to want to let go of her. She sensed his longing and was overcome by the tenderness of his embrace.

He pulled away for a moment and looked at her. His lips parted as though he wanted to say something to her. He cast his gaze downward and pulled her back into a hug that completely enveloped her.

It didn't matter to her if he couldn't express what he was feeling. The power of the kiss and the tenderness of his embrace spoke volumes to her.

I could stay in his arms forever.

The sweetness of the moment was broken by the sound of the doorbell ringing.

ELEVEN

Trevor was still reeling from the sweetness of Valerie's kiss when he opened the door and saw one of the officers who had been involved in the search.

"We found Lexi in the brush by the river. She's alive, but highly unresponsive. They are taking her over to Dr. Mills."

Valerie, who stood behind him, gasped.

"Thanks...we'll get over there as fast as we can," Trevor said.

He closed the door and turned to face Valerie. All the color had drained from her face, and the look in her eyes was frantic.

"I can go check on her if you need to stay with Bethany," he offered.

The enchantment of the kiss faded as

harsh reality barged into his awareness. Valerie's life was still under threat. She wasn't safe. The syndicate may have killed her dog.

Valerie turned one way and then the other. "I can ummm…" She held a trembling hand to her lips, then let out a breath and straightened her shoulders. "I can call Mrs. Witherspoon in a little bit. She's supposed to come over today, anyway. I forgot to cancel her after McNeal told me to take sick leave."

As he watched her struggle with the decision, he was filled with compassion. "Hey." He grabbed her delicate hand and pressed it between his. He wanted to tell her that Lexi was going to be okay, but that might be a lie. He moved toward her, brushed a strand of hair out of her eyes and kissed her forehead. "I'll wait with you, and we'll go together to see Lexi."

Once Mrs. Witherspoon showed up, they sped across town toward the vet clinic.

"Which way?" Trevor glanced over at her.

Her fingers were laced tightly together and resting in her lap. Her lips were pressed into a hard, straight line. Nothing he could say to her would take away the worry. All he could do was walk through it with her.

"Take a left at this next street," she said, releasing a heavy sigh.

As he drove, he saw signs that indicated an area called the Lost Woods was close by. The vet clinic was set off by itself on a large piece of land. Two horses, one with a bandage on its leg, ate grass in a fenced field next to the stark white building. Valerie jumped out of the car almost before Trevor had come to a stop. He followed behind her.

Valerie rushed over to the woman behind the counter. "There was a police K-9 brought in just a little bit ago?"

"Oh, sure, Dr. Mills is just back there with her now." The receptionist pointed to a door behind her.

Trevor followed as Valerie pushed through the door. Dr. Mills was a slen-

der fiftyish woman with pronounced eyebrows and candy-apple-red hair pulled
back in a bun.

Valerie stopped short when she saw
Lexi lying on the sterile, metal exam
table. She shuddered. Trevor came up
from behind, wrapping his arms around
her.

Valerie glanced from the prone dog to
the vet. "How is she?"

Lexi managed a tail wag at the sound
of Valerie's voice.

"She's becoming more responsive. The
wagging tail is a good sign." The doctor
put the half glasses she had on a string
on her face.

Valerie stepped toward the exam table
and rubbed Lexi's ears.

"What happened to her?" Trevor asked.

Valerie bent her head close to Lexi's ear
and made soothing noises while she pet-
ted her. Her eyes glazed as she stroked
the dog's belly.

"The department ordered a tox screen
on her, but my guess is she was given

some kind of drug that paralyzed her. She's just now starting to show movement in her extremities."

Valerie didn't look up from the dog. "The drug wears off after a while?" She held her hand close to the dog's mouth. Lexi licked her fingers.

"If that's what it is, she should have a full recovery." The vet leaned toward the dog, touching her front flank. "There's some barbs in her fur consistent with the use of a taser."

Valerie shook her head. "That would be the only way they would have been able to drug her in the first place." Her voice tinged with anger as she stroked Lexi's head. "I can't believe they did this to her."

"Can Valerie take her home?"

Dr. Mills stuck her hand in the pocket of her white lab coat. "I'd like to watch her for a couple more hours until the drug wears off completely."

Valerie straightened her back. She bit her lower lip and turned her head away. Trevor's ire rose over what had been done to Lexi. How dare the syndicate put Valerie through this emotional turmoil.

"You're welcome to stay with her for a little bit, but she needs to rest." The doctor pulled a chart off a wall. "I've got a sick parakeet to look after." She left the room.

Valerie looked at Trevor. "If it's all right with you, I'd like to be alone with Lexi."

"Sure," Trevor said, trying to hide his disappointment. He wanted to be with them, but he needed to honor her wishes. He left the exam room and found a seat in the waiting room. Valerie and Lexi were a tight team, partners, and he wasn't a part of that. Despite the kiss, he was still the outsider.

Valerie emerged from the exam room about twenty minutes later. Her eyes were red from crying.

Trevor struggled to find words to comfort her. What could he say to make her feel better? As they stepped out into the parking lot, his rage over what the Serpent had done returned. The syndicate represented the worst kind of evil, and now they were trying to get at Valerie while she was in her home.

Once they were in the car, Trevor put the key in the ignition. "You want me to take you back home?"

"I'm going to call McNeal and see if he has changed his mind. I don't like being on the sidelines like this. If I can work the streets, maybe I can take this syndicate apart piece by piece." The ire he heard in her voice was the same that he had felt. But her drive to make a difference was overshadowing her sense of self-preservation.

"Valerie, I've been thinking... After what happened last night, maybe it's not good for you to stay at your house." Trevor pulled out of the parking lot.

"I can't go to my parents'. That would put their lives in danger, too. My dad has his hands full taking care of my mother. Maybe I could stay with Lucy or one of my brothers."

He shook his head. "You need something with a higher level of security. Maybe the department can set up a safe house for you."

Her voice rose half an octave. "So then I become the prisoner. I can't work, and I can't be in my own home. It could be months before we bring the Serpent in."

"The Serpent's ability to get at you seems to be escalating." He only wanted to keep her safe. His protection and what the department could manage didn't seem to be enough.

She rubbed her temple as her voice gave way to frustration. "Bethany is just starting to adjust to all the changes. She'd be in a new strange place again and have to adjust all over." She ran her hands through her hair. "I understand what you are saying, I do, but I just…" Valerie turned away and stared out the window.

Trevor took a moment to gather his thoughts before speaking. He checked his rearview mirror. Only one dark-colored car was behind him on the long stretch of country road.

He understood her point of view, but his desperation to protect her pressed in on him from all sides. "Maybe it would be best if McNeal extended your sick leave for a while."

"I want to do my job. I want to get these guys out of Sagebrush. If you two want to lock me up in some stuffy safe house all day, it's like the syndicate has already won. Do you think I can't do my job?"

"Valerie, that's not what I meant." Trevor felt like he was slipping down an icy wall. Valerie thought he was insulting her ability to do her job. Frustration over not being able to shield her from harm gnawed at him.

He'd been so intent on their conversation he hadn't noticed that the dark-colored car behind him had pulled up beside them without passing. When he looked over, he saw Derek Murke's leering face as he raised a pistol and aimed at Trevor's window.

Trevor swerved, and the shot went wild.

Valerie screamed and ducked beneath the dashboard.

Trevor accelerated and checked his rear-view mirror. The car was behind them but closing in fast.

Trevor turned onto a dirt road just as Murke's bumper hit his. Another shot shattered the back window. Then he heard an odd popping sound. The dirt road was surrounded by trees on both sides. He sped up, creating a dust cloud that made it hard to gauge where Murke was.

His car fishtailed and then vibrated. Now he knew what that popping sound had been. Murke had shot out a back tire. He braked with force, causing the car to spin in a half circle. They weren't going to get anywhere on a bald tire.

"Get out." He pushed his door open.

As the dust cloud settled, he could see Murke's car careening toward them. He ran around to Valerie's side of the car where she crouched low. He grabbed her hand. Murke got out of his car and ran toward them. Trevor pulled his gun and fired a shot. They'd find cover in the trees thirty yards away if they could make it without being hit. Pulling Valerie with him, he ran. Murke stalked toward them. He'd have to get pretty close to have any accuracy with a pistol.

They were ten yards from the trees. Trevor stole a glance toward Murke as he lifted his gun. He dove to the ground and scrambled toward the trees. Valerie stayed low, as well. The pistol shot he'd braced for never happened.

A panicked look spread across Murke's face as he stared down at his gun. He was out of bullets. He raced back to his car.

This was his chance to take Murke into custody before he drove away. He turned to Valerie. "Hide in the trees. Wait for me."

"No way! I'm coming with you."

"You're unarmed," he growled. "You need to lay low. And besides, you have Bethany to consider…"

Valerie's eyes clouded over, but she obeyed without protest. He could see the yellow of her jacket as she stepped behind a cluster of trees.

Murke crawled back in his car and disappeared beneath the dash. Trevor ran toward the car, ready to shoot. This was his chance. He could get Murke.

Murke popped his head up behind the steering wheel and lifted a rifle, aiming it in Trevor's direction.

Trevor hit the ground and then soldier-crawled toward the cover of the trees. His pistol was no match for a rifle. A shot zinged over his back. Murke's footsteps pounded hard ground.

When he entered the trees, Valerie found him and pulled him to his feet. They ran deeper into the Lost Woods as shot after shot reverberated around them, breaking branches and stirring up dust.

With no clearly defined trail in front of them, they pushed through the thick underbrush and trees. He held on tight to Valerie's hand. Another shot rang out, and a branch above them broke. Murke was gaining on them.

They zigzagged through more trees, their feet pounding the dusty earth, both of them growing breathless from exertion. When twenty minutes passed without any indication that Murke was still close by, Trevor stopped, taking in a raspy breath. Valerie pressed close to his back.

"It looks like Murke is playing offense and has decided to take me out of the equation," Trevor said.

Valerie nodded. "This score he told his half sister about must be pretty big for him to take this kind of a risk." She leaned over, placing her hands on her knees and drawing in deep breaths.

All the trees around him looked exactly alike. "How do we get back to the main road?"

Valerie shook her head, turning in one direction and then the other. "I have no idea."

Going back to the car wasn't a viable option. He didn't have a spare, and trying to drive with a bad tire would just make them an easy target for Murke. He pulled his cell phone off his belt. No reception. He had to find a way to turn this thing around and take Murke down, but how?

"Let's just keep moving in the general direction of the main road. We got to come to it sooner or later." She placed her hand in his.

Despite their earlier fight…despite snapping at him for suggesting the safe house and forgoing her job…Valerie trusted him enough to lead her out of the Lost Woods.

As they started running again, he prayed that trust wasn't misplaced.

TWELVE

Valerie's leg muscles burned from running, and her lungs felt like they had been scraped with a steak knife. Her throat was parched.

Trevor continued to lead them through the woods, but every bunch of trees looked like the one before. They might even be going in circles. They risked running around a cluster of trees and ending up face-to-face with Murke.

She had to get her bearings, had to obtain some sense of direction. There was a reason these were called the Lost Woods. She'd heard the stories of people who went in and never came out. The thick undergrowth and trees were like a maze.

Trevor stopped. "I've got one bullet

left," he said, clicking the magazine out of his gun. "Murke has outmatched us firepower-wise, but maybe we can still catch him."

Valerie swallowed, trying to produce some moisture in her mouth. It felt like she had swallowed dust. How much longer could they keep this up? "Maybe we should just try to get back to the main road."

Trevor glanced at his phone panel again. "If I could get some cell reception, we could get backup out here. Murke wouldn't be able to leave these woods."

Murke could be lying in wait for them around any corner. How on earth would they catch him? Valerie studied her surroundings. They'd been running for at least half an hour. She wasn't so sure they could even find their way back to the car if they had to.

They heard voices, two men exchanging verbal jabs and raucous laughter.

"Maybe we'll get some help." Trevor's voice tinged with hope.

As the conversation carried over the trees, something about the way the men talked seemed menacing. "I'm not so sure about that. Let's hide." She pulled on his shirt and then slipped behind some thick undergrowth.

He hit the ground and scooted toward her. "What are we doing?"

"Lot of drug deals go down here and lots of transients hang out here, too," she whispered. "Let's see if we can get a read on these guys before we go asking for help."

She lay close enough to Trevor to feel his body heat. His soapy-clean scent mixed with sweat. Despite the fear coursing through her, his closeness calmed her.

The voices of the two men grew distant and then loud again. As their conversation became more distinct, it was obvious that they had been drinking. They could have been on a bender and been out here for days. There was no guarantee they even had a car. They might have hitchhiked and been dropped off, or come from one of the low-rent housing districts that were close to the woods.

As the men passed within twenty feet of them, Trevor turned to look at her, rolling his eyes. He was probably thinking the same thing. Not the rescue party they were hoping for.

When the voices faded, they crawled out from under the bush. Valerie dusted off her pants. It had been a while since they had seen or heard any sign that Murke was close. Maybe he had given up or gotten lost himself. She reached out for Trevor's hand, but he didn't notice.

Now that the threat from Murke had died down, she could feel the wedge between them again, probably over their fight. Trevor had been so great in helping with Bethany, and the kiss had been wonderful, but he seemed to be closing down again. His feelings for her were even more unclear.

He walked with his back to her, talking over his shoulder. "What kind of drug deals take place out here?"

If he only felt comfortable talking about work, she would talk about work. "It's one of the syndicate's favorite places to do business. It's a hard place to patrol. We usually know something has gone wrong when we find a body."

She stared at his back as the emotional chasm between them seemed to grow. Was he just preoccupied with dealing with Murke?

She scurried to catch up. "Captain McNeal thinks that Rio was taken because the syndicate needs him to find something that is hidden out here."

"Really?" Only half his attention was on the conversation as he turned in one direction and then another.

All around her, the trees and boulders looked the same. She struggled to shake off that sinking feeling. They were lost. "Maybe we should try to get back to the car. We can navigate our way out from the road."

He stopped and looked directly at her. "Good idea. Which way would that be?"

She turned a half circle until her gaze traveled up toward a high rock formation. She caught movement on top of the rock. An instant after it registered that what she was seeing was a man holding a gun, she heard the zing of a rifle being fired.

Trevor pulled her to the ground, shielding her with his arm. They crawled behind a boulder.

Trevor spoke into her ear. "We know where he is at now. I'm going to see if I can sneak up on him."

She grabbed his sleeve. "Trevor, I don't know if that is a good idea." He was down to only one bullet. He'd be walking into a death trap.

"He's got to come down off that rock sooner or later...and I'll be ready for him." He pulled his cell phone off his belt. "Keep trying to get some reception. Backup would be nice, but if I have to do this myself, I will."

Staying low and moving quickly, he disappeared into the brush. Valerie beat down the approaching sense of doom.

Maybe Trevor could succeed. She hadn't had time to notice if there was brush around the boulder Murke had climbed onto. There might be a place for him to hide.

After slipping out of her yellow coat, which made her too easy to see, she angled around the thick brush where they had found shelter. She spread the coat over a bush, so it would serve as a decoy.

Valerie soldier-crawled on the ground until a rock outcropping came into view. The rock formation was at least twenty feet high. Cell reception might be better up there, and it would allow her a view of the landscape. Pushing aside the worries about Trevor that plagued her, she found a foothold and climbed up to a flat spot. A finger-shaped rock that was higher than the flat spot shielded her from view on one side.

She craned her neck around the rock. She could see the boulder where Murke was perched. Though the sniper's movements were small, she caught the glint of his rifle barrel in the noonday sun. When she scanned the surrounding area, she saw no sign of Trevor.

Dear God, keep him safe.

She checked the phone and breathed a sigh of relief. She had a signal. Dispatch promised to send three patrol cars, but she could only give them a rough idea of where they were at in the Lost Woods.

The dispatcher's voice came across the line strong and clear. "Then we'll probably have to send a chopper, too."

Valerie hung up. It would take at least twenty minutes for the units to mobilize and get out here. She peered out at the landscape again. Murke was crawling down from the boulder. Where was Trevor?

Murke stopped and looked in her direction. She swung around and pressed hard against the finger-shaped rock. Had he seen her?

With her heart racing, she rolled over on her stomach and peered out. She still saw no sign of Trevor. Had he even made it over to the boulder? The view from high up made the layout clear, but it would be easy enough to get turned around if you were on the ground.

Valerie heard branches breaking some distance from her. Several deer jumped out of the brush and bounded toward a clearing. She caught a flash of movement not too far from where the deer had been. That had to be Trevor.

A rifle shot shattered the stillness. Murke had spotted the yellow coat and taken aim. The shot reverberated off the cliffs and rocks. The deer scattered, their hooves pounding hard earth. Valerie had a clear view of the action below. She gasped.

Trevor had mistaken the echo of the rifle for the rifle shot and was headed in the wrong direction, but that was not what had sent a charge of fear through her. Murke was stalking toward where Trevor had been. It was only a matter of time before Murke saw Trevor.

As Murke closed in on Trevor, Valerie's heart seized up. She couldn't cry out. That would put both of them in jeopardy. Murke drew closer to the rock where she hid. Murke kept looking through the sight of his rifle. He must have spotted Trevor moving through the brush and was trying to line up a shot.

Murke was almost even with the rock where Valerie hid. She had only one option to stop him and a split second in which to do it. She peered out behind the outcropping and waited until Murke was directly below her.

Valerie leapt from the rock, landing on top of Murke and taking him to the ground. The rifle fell from his hand. Valerie struggled to get Murke into a hold by immobilizing his neck. Murke swung free of her grasp and reached out to hit her. She angled away, grabbed his foot and pulled him to the ground.

Murke let out a groan, showing his teeth. The sneer on his face communicated pure hatred. He meant to kill her.

He leapt toward her, hands curled like claws.

Trevor came up behind him and wrestled Murke to the ground.

Sirens sounded in the distance, and the mechanical hum of a helicopter grew louder.

Murke twisted and writhed and cursed, but Trevor held him down face-first.

Valerie tore the heavy-duty laces from her boots. "Tie him up with these. They'll hold until backup gets here."

Within minutes, the helicopter was low to the ground and directly overhead. The sirens grew closer. The helicopter must have alerted the police cars to their position.

Trevor placed a knee on the small of Murke's back to keep him from moving. He looked up at Valerie. Gratitude colored his voice as his mouth turned up in a smile. "Thanks...you saved my life."

"It's what partners do for each other." However, what she had done was more than just one lawman looking out for another. She cared about Trevor.

"You could have died. You didn't have to do that for me." The tenderness in his eyes made her heart flutter.

"Your life was worth saving." She looked at him for a long moment, expecting him to say more. His gaze rested on her, but he remained silent. What words had gone unspoken between them? What was he thinking?

"You're hurting me." Murke cursed and struggled beneath the weight of Trevor's knee. Trevor focused his attention on making sure the fugitive stayed put. Valerie picked up the rifle and kept it trained on Murke until help arrived.

About twenty minutes passed before the first of several officers emerged through the trees. One of the officers pulled his handcuffs from his tool belt. Trevor stood up, his hand on his gun while the officer cuffed Murke and pulled him to his feet.

Trevor spoke to the officer who had cuffed Murke. "I want to interview him as soon as he is processed. He's got a lot of questions to answer."

Murke looked at Trevor with his dark soulless eyes and then spat on the ground before being led away.

As she watched Murke being escorted through the trees, a sense of satisfaction swept over her. Trevor had his fugitive.

Detective Jackson Worth emerged through the trees with Titan taking up the lead. The lab's black fur shone in the sun. Seeing Titan was a sad reminder that her own K-9 partner was not with her.

Jackson held out a hand to Trevor. "Job well done. They are going to take him in the chopper to get him to the station faster." He shook Valerie's hand, as well. "I saw what he did to your car. I bet you two could use a ride back into town."

Trevor nodded. "I suppose I will have to make arrangements for my car to be towed." With Jackson and Titan in the lead, Trevor and Valerie followed, pushing brush out of the way until the dirt road came into view.

"I'd like to swing by Doc Mills's place and see if Lexi is ready to come home," Valerie said as she walked beside Trevor.

"Consider it done," Jackson replied.

"I need to be dropped off at the station," Trevor said. "So I can find out what this big score is that was Murke's undoing."

Trevor's words brought her frustration to the surface. She couldn't be a part of that questioning, not as long as McNeal had her on forced sick leave.

Trevor must have sensed her disappointment. He reached over and touched her hand, squeezing her fingers. With Murke in custody, it would only be a matter of days or even hours before Trevor returned to San Antonio. She might never see him again.

They drove along the road that bordered the Lost Woods back to the vet clinic. Jackson had barely stopped the patrol car when Valerie pushed open the door and rushed into the clinic.

Doctor Mills's assistant stood behind the tall counter. Recognition spread across her face when she saw Valerie. "She's in the kennels out back. You are free to take her home."

Valerie rushed down the long hallway and pushed through the door. The first kennel had a collie with a cone around its neck and the second was empty. She found Lexi lying down in the third kennel. The dog leapt to her feet and trotted over to Valerie. She stood up on her hind paws, resting her front paws on the chainlink fence.

Bursting with joy, Valerie leaned down so Lexi could kiss her face. "I missed you." The dog's face with the light brown markings above her eyes and the head tilted sideways communicated love. She wrapped her hands around Lexi's thick neck.

Dr. Mills came and stood by the back entrance. "You might want to walk her around a little bit, let her get her land legs back. We just put her out in the kennel a few minutes ago."

Valerie took the leash from Dr. Mills and opened the gate. "Lex, come."

The dog looked up at her, but didn't move. Then she bowed her head. Valerie thought her heart would break. Lexi had been traumatized by what she had been through.

Trevor came and stood at the edge of the building. "We should get going. I've got to make arrangements for Murke to be transported back to San Antonio."

Valerie stepped into the kennel. "Can you just give me a few minutes? Lexi is still not herself." Her voice faltered. Seeing her strong, brave dog cower because of the abuse she had endured tore Valerie to pieces. "I can get a ride into town some other way if you're in a hurry."

Trevor put his hands in his pockets. "No, we can wait." His voice filled with compassion. "Take all the time you need."

She clicked Lexi into the leash and pulled. Lexi obeyed, but the confidence she had always seen with Lexi seemed to be deflated. The dog hung her head as Valerie led her around the field by the clinic.

Valerie dropped to her knees and wrapped her arms around the dog's neck. Lexi's coarse fur was warm against her skin. "What did they do to you?"

The dog licked her cheek as though to reassure her that everything would be okay. Valerie pulled back and rubbed Lexi's velvety ears. Dark brown eyes looked back at her. "We'll get through this together."

She took in a breath and rose to her feet. Valerie worked with her a little longer, hoping to see some of Lexi's tenacious spirit return. Though she obeyed the commands, the drive that had made Lexi such a great K-9 wasn't there.

Valerie glanced over her shoulder where Trevor had been watching at a distance.

She moved toward him. "I know…we need to get going."

Trevor seemed to be all business now that Murke was caught. Had the kiss meant anything to him? She longed for an opportunity to be alone with him to talk before he left, but she didn't see how that would happen.

Valerie rode in the back of the patrol car with Titan beside her and Lexi on her lap. She didn't mind. It felt good to have Lexi close. Holding the dog might even help with her emotional recovery.

Jackson turned onto the street where she lived. Her heart sank. She might be saying good-bye to Trevor for the last time. He turned his head sideways but didn't look at her from the front seat. He hadn't said much of anything since catching Murke.

As they pulled up, she was surprised to see Captain McNeal standing on the sidewalk by her house. The expression on his face was grim, and his shoulders bent forward.

What was going on here?

THIRTEEN

Anxiety stabbed at Trevor's nerves as Jackson pulled up to the curb. McNeal had come over to Valerie's house instead of meeting him at the station. Something pretty serious must be going down.

Trevor got out of the passenger seat and hurried to open the back door for Valerie. She looked up at him, her round, green eyes filled with trust. Heartache over having to say goodbye to her had made it hard for him to say anything at all to her. It didn't make sense that their lives should go on in separate directions and yet, he was afraid to tell her how he felt about her. What if the feelings weren't mutual?

Lexi jumped out of the backseat first. The dog seemed to be perking up a little, though he had yet to see that bobbed tail wag with enthusiasm. He took Valerie's hand and helped her up to the sidewalk.

Jackson got out of the driver's seat and rested his forearm on the top of the police car. "I've got to get back to work. Take care of Lexi, Valerie."

She nodded as Jackson got back into the white SUV and drove off.

McNeal strode toward them. "I'll spare you the small talk. Murke escaped. Once the chopper landed, he overpowered the two officers who were escorting him to processing."

The news was like a boulder slamming against Trevor's chest. "Did he have help?"

"I don't think he had inside help. But someone picked him up on the street once he got away." McNeal shifted his weight and rested his hands on his hips. "When you didn't show up at the police station, I figured you were here with Valerie. I wanted you to get the news in person."

"We stopped to get Lexi," Valerie explained.

A mixture of frustration and despair wrestled within Trevor as he struggled to find solutions to getting Murke back into custody. How could this have happened? "I assume you have units out looking for him?"

McNeal nodded.

Valerie stepped forward. "It's going to take more than patrol units to find Murke. We have to be strategic about where we look."

McNeal turned toward Valerie. "You two have been working this case together, and I'll take any input you have, Valerie. But I still don't feel comfortable putting you back out on the street."

Valerie's jaw went slack as a veil of disappointment shrouded her eyes, but she lifted her head and squared her shoulders as a show of acceptance like the true professional she was.

"With all due respect, sir, the syndicate is going to get at Valerie no matter where she is," Trevor said. "They almost got into her home last night. Valerie is the reason we even got Murke into custody in the first place. She risked her life to save mine." He scrubbed a hand across his face. "Now that Murke has decided taking me out of the equation is the solution to his problems, there is no one I would rather have my back than Officer Salgado."

Valerie's face glowed with gratitude.

Raising his eyebrows, McNeal glanced over at Valerie and then rested his gaze back on Trevor.

Trevor feared he had overstepped the boundaries of McNeal's authority, but he had meant every word he said. Locking Valerie away wasn't going to make her any safer and being overly protective of her wouldn't bring back Agent Cory Smith. The syndicate had ways of getting to her no matter what. Valerie was ten times the professional Cory had been. She'd shown herself for the fearless and quick-thinking cop she was out in the Lost Woods.

McNeal cleared his throat. "Well…your point is valid. She's vulnerable staying at home, too, and she's an asset in catching Murke. I'd feel better about putting Valerie back out on the street if you were with her. Once you go back to San Antonio, I'll reassess."

Valerie grabbed McNeal's hand and shook it vigorously. "Thank you, sir."

"For now, the two of you need to focus on finding Murke," McNeal said. "We'll figure out the extent to which you can resume your patrol duties later."

"Yes, sir," said Trevor.

"I got to get back to the station." McNeal ambled toward his car where Chief perched faithfully in the backseat.

Valerie turned toward Trevor and mouthed the words "Thank you" as McNeal drove away. The look on her face and the warmth in her eyes were captivating. There was so much more he wanted to say to her, but now was not the time. "So what is your theory about where we'll find Murke?"

"We backtrack to where we know he has been. We know he has had contact with Leroy Seville, as well as his half sister, and someone had to have sold him those guns."

The half sister and Leroy seemed like dead ends. Murke had burned his bridges with them. It could take days to track down whoever had sold Murke the guns. His mind went through the catalog of Murke's known movements. If only they knew what this big score was that Murke was after.

"What about Arianna's Diner? Maybe he said something to the waitstaff or was meeting someone there," Valerie said.

Trevor lifted his head. "It's worth a try."

"Let me just go inside and give Bethany a hug and then we can get going." Valerie turned and headed up the sidewalk.

"I'll come with you…if you want." He wanted to make sure Bethany had made a full recovery as much as she did.

"That would be nice," she said softly.

He stepped into line a few paces behind her. "Valerie?"

"Yes." She looked over her shoulder, offering him a smile that melted his heart.

"It's good to be working with you again."

"You, too."

Valerie pushed open the door. Mrs. Witherspoon and Bethany were sitting on the couch reading a storybook. Bethany burst out in a smile when she saw Trevor. The surge of joy he felt at such a small gesture surprised him.

With Mrs. Witherspoon's assurances that Bethany's fever had not returned, Valerie felt comfortable going. At Stella's request, Bethany opened her mouth and showed everyone where a tooth had poked through her gum.

After getting back into uniform, Valerie drove with Trevor and Lexi to the station to get the patrol car.

Arianna's Diner was on the main floor of a large brick building in downtown

Sagebrush. The decor featured distressed wood floors, soft lighting and a tin ceiling. Though the restaurant was known for its coffee and pastries, it also served sandwiches and light Italian dishes.

At this time of day between the lunch and dinner hours, the diner was virtually abandoned. A waiter stood at the corner of a counter folding silverware into napkins. A fan whirred on the tin ceiling.

Only two customers sat at separate tables, a college-age girl with a cup of coffee and an open journal and an older man enjoying a plate of pasta.

Trevor walked in behind Valerie. "Do you eat here ever?"

"Lots of the officers stop here because it's on the way to the station, but I think I've only been in here once or twice," Valerie said.

They were really grasping at straws to come back here, but Trevor had vowed not to leave Sagebrush without Murke in custody. Thin leads were enough to keep him hoping. He could sense the clock ticking

Sharon Dunn   259

though. Would the big score Murke had told his half sister about be enough to keep him here now that the law had managed to catch him once? However clever Murke was at escape, he had to be shaking in his shoes over being taken into custody.

When they walked across the diner floor, the waiter at the counter lifted his head. "Yes, may I help you?"

Trevor waited for Valerie to take the lead.

"We have some questions to ask you about a man who was in here a few days ago." She pulled Murke's picture out of her pocket and laid it on the counter.

The man stared down at the picture. Trevor tensed when the waiter shook his head.

"What day would he have been in here?" the waiter asked, looking back at them.

"Tuesday afternoon."

"I wasn't on shift that day. Maryanne might have been. Just a minute. I don't think she has left yet." He disappeared behind a swinging door.

Trevor studied the restaurant walls, which were decorated with photographs and fifties memorabilia.

A moment later, the waiter returned with a plump, forty-something woman with bouffant blond hair. Dark eyeliner rimmed her eyes. "So y'all are wonderin' about a feller who came in on Tuesday." She raised an eyebrow at them. "Honey, do you have any idea how many customers stomp through here in a day?"

Her comment was a bleak reminder of how thin the lead was.

Valerie pushed the photograph across the counter. The woman glanced at it, shook her head and then looked away.

Disappointment fell on Trevor like a lead blanket. The woman stopped as she was turning to go back to the kitchen. She angled back toward the counter and picked up the photo again, nodding slowly.

"Actually...I *do* remember him. We were

really busy that day, but this guy wanted to talk to the boss."

"The boss?" Valerie stepped closer to the counter.

Maryanne put her hand on her hip. "Arianna Munson—she owns the place."

"Is Arianna here now?" Trevor shifted his weight, excitement colored his voice.

"She only comes in once in a while to make sure everything is running smoothly." Maryanne made a face. "Arianna's good at the business end of things but not so good with the customers."

"Can we get an address for her?" Valerie asked.

"Sure." Maryanne pulled a pen from behind her ear and grabbed a paper napkin. She talked as she wrote. "I don't know what they talked about in her office, but Arianna was white as a ghost when she came out."

Was it possible that Arianna was the girlfriend that Murke had wanted to get even with?

Trevor stepped toward the counter. "Did

she say anything to you about the meeting?"

"Hard to say. She's not exactly a woman who's in touch with her feelings." The waitress shrugged her shoulders. "She was just crabbier than usual with the chef and waitstaff for the rest of the day." She pushed the napkin with the address on it toward Valerie.

"Thank you for all your help." Trevor felt a lightness in his step as they headed out the door toward Valerie's patrol car. If Arianna was the old girlfriend, she might be able to answer a lot of questions for them. She might even know where Murke was.

Valerie checked the address before handing the napkin to Trevor. "It won't take us but ten minutes to get there."

Valerie adhered to the speed limit through downtown and turned off on a wide street that featured luxury high-rises and lots of greenery. The Mercedes and BMWs parked on the street indicated that the neighborhood was high income.

Valerie pulled over to the curb and pointed. "She's in the Merill building. It used to be a fancy hotel, but it's been converted to high-end apartments."

"Restaurant business must be doing her pretty good," Trevor mused.

They entered the lobby, which featured a marble floor and wide, sweeping staircase. Valerie pointed toward the elevators. "Fifth floor."

They stepped inside, waited for the doors to close and pushed the button for the fifth floor. Trevor could feel his anticipation growing as the number three and then four lit up on the panel. "Maybe we'll get some answers from this woman."

Valerie nodded.

The doors swung open. At the end of the hall, a woman in a white coat with her back to them stood holding a suitcase and sticking a key into a doorknob.

When she turned around, Valerie gasped, her eyes going wide with recognition.

"The Serpent," she whispered.

FOURTEEN

The shock of seeing the Serpent was like being plunged into ice water. Valerie struggled for a deep breath as her hand went for her gun. Arianna and the Serpent were one and the same.

"Stop. FBI." Trevor ran down the hall with his gun drawn.

The woman dropped her suitcase, dashed inside the apartment and slammed the door. As Valerie ran behind Trevor, she could hear a locking bolt sliding into place.

Trevor pounded on the door. "Ma'am, we need to talk to you." He waited only a second before lifting his leg to kick the door in. The first kick only shook the door.

"I don't hear anything. She might have a back exit from the apartment." Adrenaline coursed through her. "I'll go down to the ground floor and see if I can catch her."

Trevor grabbed her arm. "No, I can't let you. This woman wants you dead. We don't know if she's armed or not."

"But Trevor…"

He kicked the door a second time, splintering it off its hinges. He grabbed her hand. "You're staying with me."

They entered a huge living room done mostly in white. While Trevor searched the room, Valerie ran to the window. A large parking garage was across the street.

Trevor shouted from a second room. "This way!"

She ran to a back entryway where Trevor stood by an open door with steps that led down.

When they were halfway down the exterior stairs, Valerie scanned the area below them. Arianna was weaving her way through the cars in the lot toward the parking garage, her white coat easy to spot among the darker cars.

They reached the bottom of the stairs just as Arianna disappeared into the parking garage.

"I'll grab Lexi." While Trevor headed toward the parking garage, Valerie ran the short distance to the patrol vehicle and opened the back door. "Lexi, come."

The dog leapt out of the car and bolted toward Valerie. Valerie grabbed the long canvas leash and commanded, "Get her. Get her."

The light diminished by half when they entered the dark cave of the parking garage. The dog pulled hard, making her way past the parked cars, her ears back and her nose low to the ground. People who were being chased put out an unusual amount of adrenaline. Lexi's nose was sensitive to pick up on the scent.

Valerie glanced up ahead, hoping to see Trevor. Toward the entrance of the garage, a car started up and pulled out of its space. Lexi moved in the opposite direction. She'd trust the dog's nose over any theory she might have. She was confident the car leaving the garage was not Arianna's.

Approaching footsteps seemed to echo. A moment later, Trevor came around a curve. He held his gun in his hand and spoke between ragged breaths. "No sign of her yet."

"I'll call and see if I can get another unit to watch the exit. I don't think she has left here. She's got to be hiding in her car or somewhere in this garage. Lexi will find her."

The dog pulled hard, stopped for a moment, retracing her steps. When she finally picked up the scent, she made yipping sounds that suggested extreme excitement.

Using her shoulder mic, Valerie radioed in for backup to block the exit. Lexi stopped, lifting her head and sniffing the air. She ran ten yards in one direction and then ten in the opposite.

"What's going on?"

The leash went slack. "She's lost the scent. She'll find it again."

Lexi continued to sniff the ground, but not as frantically. Both of them slowed their pace. Valerie listened for footsteps but didn't hear any.

"What do we got here?" Trevor turned side to side. "Three stories of cars."

Valerie ran over to the elevator that lead to the higher floors. The elevator wasn't in operation, and Lexi didn't alert to anything outside the doors. "She's still on this floor. She has to be."

They walked, catching their breath and listening for the sound of a car engine starting up or lights turning on. With Valerie at her heels, Lexi wove through the cars. Arianna must have crouched and used the cars as cover on the way to her own car. She probably ditched the white coat, too.

Trevor lifted his gun and edged toward

Valerie. "Stay close to me—she might see this as an opportunity to take you out."

Valerie tensed. Trevor was right; she could be walking into an ambush. The woman had clearly recognized her. After all her efforts at sending henchmen to do her dirty work, the Serpent probably would have no qualms about finishing the job herself.

Lexi's yipping and sniffing vocalizations grew more intense. She pulled hard on the leash again. "She's got it. She's close." Valerie let go of the leash. "Get her, get her."

They ran past several compact cars then turned at a circular angle leading upward. Lexi had separated from them and was running hard. Tires screeched on concrete as a car backed out of its space. Lexi yelped. Valerie couldn't see her dog behind the car. Had she been hit?

In an instant, the roar of an engine surrounded Valerie. Terror invaded every muscle as headlights blinded her. She froze. Trevor's arms surrounded her, lifting her off her feet. Her body impacted with the hood of a car, and they rolled over the top and onto the concrete. Arianna's car screeched, taking a hard turn as it roared through the parking garage.

Arianna had used her one chance to kill Valerie and now she was focused on getting away.

Trevor helped her to her feet. "You all right?"

Lexi. She had to get to Lexi. Half stumbling and half running, she made her way up the ramp. Was her partner lying run over in a pool of blood? She couldn't see anything. Couldn't hear anything.

Yelping and barking some distance away reached her ears. Relief spread through her. Lexi was okay. The sound was coming from the exit to the parking garage. That dog never gave up the chase. Valerie and Trevor ran toward the sound of the barking. They found her at the exit to the parking garage, barking and pacing up and down the sidewalk.

Valerie scanned the street. Arianna's

silver Mercedes was long gone, and Lexi was inconsolable. Valerie picked up the leash. "It's all right, girl. You did good."

Trevor touched her elbow. "You're sure you're okay?"

She nodded, barely comprehending what she'd just been through. "We lost her." She couldn't stop shaking. "I can't believe she got away." Her voice faltered.

"Hey." Trevor placed a comforting hand on her cheek. "We'll catch her. We know what the car looks like. We'll put an APB out."

The delayed reaction of what had happened finally kicked in. She'd almost died. Arianna would have crushed her under her tires like she was an insect. *Thank you, God, that I'm still alive.*

She must have given her fear away in her body language. Lexi whined and looked up at her, growing agitated.

Trevor gathered her into his arms. "It's okay to be scared."

"She could have killed me just that fast if you hadn't reacted so quickly." The warmth of his arms surrounded her. Lexi pressed against her leg but didn't object to Trevor's hug.

He held her for a long moment. She rested against his chest. His breathing, the rise and fall of his chest, surrounded her. She closed her eyes until her own heart stopped racing and her resolve returned. Now she was mad about Arianna's getting away. "Where's that backup I called for, anyway?"

Valerie radioed in the details about Arianna's car as she looked back at the entrance of the parking garage. Her gaze traveled up and down the long street and to the surrounding side streets hoping to see some sign of the silver Mercedes. Several cars passed by, but there was no sign of Arianna's car. She was long gone.

Trevor looked back toward the apartment complex. "She had a suitcase with her. She must have been planning on leaving town."

"I wonder why?" Valerie wanted to believe that the Serpent leaving meant her life could return to normal. But it was too much to hope for. Arianna would probably just give her death orders from afar. Her fear fueled her desire to catch the Serpent. She could clearly identify her now. She wanted that woman behind bars.

Trevor placed his hand on Valerie's lower back. "Let's go find out what the neighbors know."

They walked back to the apartment complex. Valerie opened the back of the patrol car for Lexi. The dog moved slower than usual. The chase had worn her out. "Lexi is still recovering. I don't want to overwork her. I think I want to take her back home and let her rest up for the day."

Trevor nodded. "Sure, we can do that." He touched her arm lightly.

Valerie was still shaken from having nearly lost her life. The warmth of Trevor's touch smoothed over much of her anxiety. He seemed to instinctually know that she needed that sense of security his nearness evoked.

They entered the back parking lot. "If

Arianna is the girlfriend Murke told his half sister about, that links him to the syndicate," Valerie said.

Trevor nodded. "I can't help but think that big score he talked about is the same thing the syndicate is looking for in the Lost Woods, the reason they took Rio."

A man in the parking lot stood by his SUV, pulling out golf clubs.

Valerie walked over to him. "Excuse me, sir, do you live in this building?"

He was an older man with a deep tan and white hair. "That's right, third floor suite." He patted his clubs. "Love being so close to the golf course."

"Do you know the lady who lives on the fifth floor...Arianna Munson."

"I know her in passing, not a very friendly lady, though." The older man picked up one of his golf clubs and twirled it in his hand. "Kind of hard to start a conversation with her. Guess she owns a swanky diner downtown?"

"When was the last time you saw her?"

"Matter of fact—" the man put the golf

club back in the bag "—I just saw her today right before I left to play a few holes."

Valerie's heart skipped a beat as she straightened her spine. "Really?"

"Sure, out here in the parking lot she was talking to a gentleman, and I tell you what, neither one of them looked none too happy."

Trevor cut a glance toward Valerie, lifting his eyebrows. He pulled the photo of Murke out of his chest pocket. "Is this the man you saw?"

The older man took the photo and stared at it for a long moment, rubbing his chin. "Yeah, that was the feller."

Valerie's anticipation grew. They'd been that close to Murke. Their trail was hot again. "Could you tell what the conversation was about?"

"I was too far away to pick up any words, even though their voices were raised. If I had to venture a guess, I would say that Arianna lady seemed afraid. This guy—" he shook the photograph

"—pointed his finger at her like he was demanding something from her. I'm tellin' ya, the lady looked really scared. Then he grabbed her arm. She got real quiet and said something that made him let go of her arm."

"How long ago would you say that was?"

The man wiped sweat from his forehead with the back of his hand and thought a moment. "I'd say an hour or two ago, I only played nine holes and there was hardly anybody else on the course."

"Thank you, sir, you've been a great help." Trevor patted the older man's shoulder.

"Always happy to lend a hand." He tilted his golf club bag, which was on wheels, and rolled it toward Merill Towers.

Valerie pieced together the information the man had given them. "Sounds like Arianna was leaving town to get away from Murke."

Trevor nodded. "I guess it's pretty clear that Murke is demanding something from

Arianna, threatening her, even. He must have found the Serpent as soon as he escaped. His desperation is growing since we are getting so close to him."

"From the way our witness describes the interaction, Arianna said something to placate him," Valerie said. "Do you suppose she knows where this big score is that the syndicate has been after, or knows how to get it for him?"

Trevor scanned the parking lot. "I'd say it's a high probability."

Valerie was surprised that news about Arianna's car hadn't come across her radio yet. A fancy car like that would be easy enough to spot. "We're only a step or two behind Murke. We ought to be able to stir up something." She walked back to the patrol car where Lexi waited just as another police car pulled up. Jackson Worth got out. The black lab Titan sat nobly in the back-seat, his chin jutting up.

"Are you the backup I called for?" It wasn't like any of the Sagebrush police to ignore a call for back up, especially Jackson.

"There was a huge drug bust on the north side. All available units were called out. Otherwise, I would have gotten here faster," Jackson said. "You said you were trying to track down guys who deal guns to people with a record. One of the perps they brought in on this drug bust is Dwayne Wilson, aka Babyface. He's known for selling guns to criminals."

Valerie perked up. Hours of work in finding someone like Dwayne Wilson had just been shortened. "You think he might have sold those guns to Murke?"

"You can question him while he's in custody," Jackson said.

"Let's get down to the station." Trevor was halfway to the patrol car.

Valerie thanked Jackson. A sense of urgency sped up her steps to the patrol car. They were two hours behind Murke in tracking him, and they knew the identity of Garry's murderer.

Once they were both inside, she started the patrol car and shifted into Reverse.

After dropping Lexi back off at the house, Valerie drove toward the station. As she pulled into the back parking lot, she couldn't help but feel that they were closing in.

FIFTEEN

Trevor stared at the door marked *Interview Room 2*. A mixture of excitement and anxiety twisted his stomach into a tight knot. They were so close to wrapping this case up. Murke had a link to the syndicate. Arianna and Serpent were one and the same.

Valerie returned from the vending machine holding the soda they would offer to Babyface, aka Dwayne Wilson, as a way of building trust. She had a file tucked under her arm.

"Why don't you take the lead on the questioning," Trevor suggested.

"Thanks!" Valerie said, appreciation evident in her tone.

She deserved it. Inside the interview

room, Dwayne Wilson sat in a hardback chair, arms crossed and chin resting on his chest. He looked up when Valerie and Trevor entered.

His street name fit. He was a chubby-cheeked man with small beady eyes and a tuft of brown hair that stuck straight up.

Valerie sat the soda on the table and slid it toward Dwayne. "Thought you might be thirsty." She took a seat while Trevor remained standing.

"I don't know why I'm even in here." Babyface tilted his chin toward the ceiling.

Valerie rested her elbows on the table and laced her fingers together. "Weren't you part of a drug bust, Dwayne?"

Babyface drew his thick eyebrows together. "I don't sell drugs. I don't do drugs."

"But you do sell guns, right?"

Trevor liked the way Valerie kept her tone neutral, even though she was making a strong accusation.

Dwayne touched his fingers to his chest.

"I'm the victim here. I was in the wrong place at the wrong time, but I wasn't doing anything bad."

Valerie flipped through the file she had brought with her. "So are you saying you weren't in the middle of some kind of gun transaction when you were picked up?"

Babyface jerked in his seat. "I was just there for a social visit."

"Really?" Trevor rested his palms on the table and leaned toward Dwayne. "We're not the guys who can put you in prison, but we are the guys who might be able to get you a lighter sentence. You being a victim of circumstance and all."

Dwayne looked squarely at Trevor. "What do you need?"

"Derek Murke," Trevor said, his heart hammering at the mention of the name.

"Who?" Dwayne looked to one side as his shoulder twitched. Body language that indicated he was lying.

Valerie slid the photo of Murke across the table. "Selling guns to a felon is pretty serious business, Dwayne."

Babyface pursed his rosebud lips and narrowed his eyes, but did not look at the photograph. He wasn't going to give in easily.

"I got to tell you, Dwayne. It doesn't look good that you were at that house with all those bad people," Trevor said.

Babyface swallowed, his Adam's apple moving up and down.

Valerie allowed for a long moment of silence, time for the man across the table to think about the charges he was facing. She flipped through the file she'd brought with her, which contained a litany of Dwayne's previous crimes. Sweat beaded on Dwayne's forehead as he looked Valerie in the eyes. The man was scared, that much was clear.

"I told you I'm not into drugs. The people at that house were in the market for some handguns. That's why I was there."

Valerie still didn't respond. She deliberately kept her face void of expression. Sometimes silence was a powerful tool.

Dwayne looked at the ceiling and let out a heavy breath. "Yeah, I know Murke."

She shifted in her chair. "Where is he staying?"

Though her voice remained even, Trevor detected a hurried quality that suggested she was as excited as he was about closing in on Murke.

Dwayne shook his head. "He's moving around a lot. I don't know." His gaze didn't waver.

Dwayne was telling the truth. Trevor's spirits deflated. Babyface wasn't going to lead them directly to Murke.

"What can you tell me about his connection to Arianna Munson?"

Valerie's questioning was tenacious and smart. He would have given up thinking Babyface could be of any use to them.

Dwayne leaned back in his chair. "She dumped him years ago and took a bunch of jewelry he had procured through illegal means. Every time I saw him he talked about getting back at her. He thinks she used the money from the jewelry to start

that restaurant and make herself all re-
spectable."

Dwayne seemed to relax a little. He
was more comfortable talking about what
Murke was up to than focusing on his
own pending legal troubles.

"So how was he going to get back at
Arianna? Is that what the gun was for?"

Dwayne shook his head. "He said the
gun was to get some Fed off his back,
so he'd have the freedom to tap into this
big score that Arianna knew about. The
way he had it figured, Arianna owed him
money."

Trevor felt a tightening through his
chest as his hand curled into a fist. He
wasn't afraid of Murke, but it made him
irate to think about how low the fugitive
would stoop to get what he wanted.

Trevor pushed himself off the wall
where he was leaning and moved back
toward the table.

Dwayne took a sip from his soda can
and licked his lips.

"When was the last time you saw

Murke?" Trevor continued to watch Dwayne's body language.

Dwayne shook his head. "I haven't seen him for a couple of days…not since I sold him the guns." He sat up straighter in his chair. "So am I free to go?"

"Not quite, but we will put in a good word for you." Valerie pushed her chair back and grabbed the file.

After they left the interrogation room, Valerie turned toward Trevor. "That narrows it down. The guns were probably to get rid of you. He's not planning some kind of robbery spree. This score he's talking about has to be the same one the syndicate is looking for, whatever it is that is hidden out in the Lost Woods."

"I just wonder what kind of information Arianna gave him. Where's he going to go next?"

Valerie shook her head. "Something Arianna would have access to or something he thinks she has access to."

"Do you suppose Murke knew Arianna was the Serpent?"

"I think he must have figured it out. Maybe that's why she was scared. She was afraid he'd blow the whistle on her," Trevor said.

Jackson came up to them outside the interrogation room. "Valerie, we just got a call that Arianna's Mercedes was found abandoned on the edge of town."

"No sign of Arianna?" Valerie's voice trembled slightly.

Jackson shook his head. "Woman like that probably has lots of resources. Somebody could have picked her up."

Valerie pulled a strand of red hair behind her ear. "The question is…did she get out of town or is she still hiding somewhere in the city?" Valerie looked up at Trevor.

She didn't need to say anything more. The fear in her eyes said it all. Whether Arianna was still in town or halfway around the world, she could still direct her thugs to take out Valerie. Now that Arianna knew that she'd been named as the Serpent, things were only going to get worse. Valerie had probably hoped for news that Arianna had been picked up and put in jail. Short of death, nothing else would make the Serpent back off.

"Also, Trevor, they towed your car in and replaced the tire." Jackson excused himself and headed back toward the desk.

Trevor checked his watch. "You're off duty in twenty minutes. I'll follow you home." His heart ached for her. He would do anything for her to feel like she was safe again.

Valerie nodded. "I just got some paperwork I need to finish up."

Half an hour later, Trevor kept an eye on the taillights of Valerie's compact car as they headed toward her place. Their lives seemed to have fallen into a routine of him escorting her home after her shift and waiting for her protection to show up. Despite the apparent safety of routine, their encounter with Arianna was a bleak reminder that Valerie was far from safe.

A black van edged between Valerie and Trevor's car. He couldn't see around it.

Traffic was too heavy to move out into the passing lane. Not having a view of her car made him nervous.

As they passed a side street, the van turned off. He breathed a sigh of relief until he looked ahead. Valerie was no longer in front of him. He checked the rearview mirror and caught a flash of red. Valerie had turned off on a street that wouldn't take her home, and the van was following her. Valerie must have suspected the van was tailing her and was trying to lose him.

Trying not to panic, he hit his blinker and turned as soon as he could. He'd have to circle back and search for them on a side street. His phone rang.

Valerie didn't wait for pleasantries. "He's following me." The strain in her voice was evident even over the phone.

Trevor's pulse raced as he gripped the phone. "I know. I'll get there as fast as I can."

"I'm parking on Sagebrush Boulevard," she said. "I'm going to get out."

"Val, wait." He wasn't so sure getting out of the vehicle was the best option.

He heard a door slam. Her words came in breathless gasps. She must be running up the street. "He has a gun. I saw him lift and aim it through the windshield when we were in traffic. That's why I turned off. There's lots of people here. I don't want to risk harming them by shooting this guy. I can hide in the crowd."

He scanned the street name as he passed it. Sagebrush Boulevard had to be close.

"I'm at this outdoor café." Her words came in a harsh whisper. "He just pulled up across the street. I'm at a back table. I don't think he can see me."

Trevor saw the sign that indicated Sagebrush Boulevard and turned off. He pressed the phone against his ear. He passed her little red car, but couldn't spot her. There were no parking spaces left. He was going to have to park on the next street. He pressed the phone hard against his ear. "Valerie?" He pulled into a space and climbed out of his sedan.

"He got out of the van. Trevor, he's walking this way."

Her voice quivered with fear. Desperate to get to her before it was too late, Trevor raced around the block and pushed through the crowds on the street. He saw two outdoor cafés on opposite sides of the street. He passed the first café. No sign of Valerie. He spotted the black van but not the would-be assailant. He must be concealing his gun in a coat or something.

Loud mariachi music poured from a Mexican restaurant as he approached the second café. Valerie was seated close to the entrance, hiding behind a menu. He recognized her shoes.

When he scanned the crowd on the street, he located the large man with dark hair. The same man who had tried to shoot Valerie at the construction site. Trevor slipped into a store entrance as the man passed by. The man walked up the street past the café.

Trevor crouched low and edged toward

where Valerie was seated. The assailant was headed up the street toward her car.

"Valerie, come on," Trevor rasped out.

He grabbed her hand and pulled her behind a crowd of people. He whispered in her ear. "He's headed up the street. We can't get to your car, but we might be able to get to mine."

It was only a matter of time before the thug turned around and started looking closer at the people on the street. The crowd cleared, and Trevor directed her toward the door of an open shop.

When he glanced over his shoulder, the assailant had turned back and was headed toward them. Recognition spread across the man's face before Trevor could duck. Hatred filled his eyes as he pushed people through the crowd, making a beeline for them.

The doors of the Mexican restaurant burst open, and revelers, complete with a mariachi band, spilled out into the street, blocking the assailant's direct path to them.

Trevor shielded Valerie as they worked their way up the street. With this many people, the sniper could shoot Valerie at point-blank range and become a face in the crowd before she hit the pavement.

Valerie pressed close to him, her arm wrapped around his waist. The thug's head towered above the others.

"This way." He held her close, directing her into an art gallery.

A college-age woman with blond spiky hair approached them in the brightly lit space. "May I help you?"

"I'm a federal agent and this woman is in danger." Trevor flashed his I.D.

"Oh, my." The woman's hand fluttered to her chest.

"Is there a back entrance we can use?" In his head, he could hear the clock ticking. How long before the assailant figured out where they had gone?

The woman shook her head.

"A window we can crawl out of?"

She pointed toward the back of the gallery. "In the storage room."

"If a big brutish man comes in here, pretend you never saw us, please," Trevor said.

He was pretty sure the clerk would be unharmed. The sniper wouldn't risk getting caught unless it meant getting his target. The woman nodded. The bell that indicated someone entering the store dinged just as Trevor closed the door to the storage room. He pushed the knob in on the door, locking it.

He could hear the shop clerk talking in that polite tone, her voice elevated slightly with fear. The thug was in the shop.

The storage room contained canvases and frames, an antique desk piled with papers and a laptop. The window was small and situated high up.

Outside the door, the woman spoke more rapidly. Trevor heard a low guttural male grunt. The man's words were indiscernible but demanding in tone.

Valerie pushed a wooden chair toward the window and flipped it open. She'd slip through fine, but it would be a tight fit for him. He boosted her up.

The doorknob shook.

"Sir, you can't go back there. That's private." Though there was an attempt at calm, the shopkeeper's voice had become more agitated.

Valerie's feet disappeared. Trevor stepped onto the chair and pulled himself up to the windowsill.

The thug pounded on the door and shook the knob again. "Get the key," he demanded.

Trevor pushed through the window, stretching out his hands so his head wouldn't hit the sidewalk. Inside, the door opened on squeaky hinges.

"See, sir, there is nobody in here," the clerk said.

On the street, Valerie helped him to his feet. He had expected to end up in an alley, but instead the street featured more shops with smaller crowds. Several people stopped to stare at him as he brushed the dust from his pants.

Trevor grabbed Valerie at the elbow. "We owe that lady a big thank you."

"At least." Valerie let out a heavy sigh, agitation evident in her expression as she pressed her lips together. "What now?"

She was shaken by what had just happened. He grabbed her hand and held it, hoping to calm her.

"We can get to my car without being spotted." Trevor stepped forward, still holding on to her hand. "We'll have to make arrangements for your car to be picked up later."

Valerie looked up and down the street. "I have a couple of friends I can call. They'll come by for the key and bring the car back."

"We better hurry. This guy is dedicated. I'm sure he's still combing the streets." Trevor glanced down at her. "Walk fast, but don't draw attention to yourself by running."

Trevor was grateful he had had to park on a side street, otherwise they'd still be evading the Serpent's thug. He opened the passenger-side door for Valerie, scanning the surrounding street as he walked over to the driver's side.

He phoned in to the police station with a description of the man who had chased him and Valerie. Maybe the Sagebrush P.D. could catch him.

Valerie was silent on the drive home. She stared out the window without focusing on anything. He knew that look, an emotional exhaustion was setting in for her. He'd seen it on witnesses he'd been assigned to protect. The constant barrage from every angle by the Serpent's henchmen was wearing on her.

When they got to her home, her nighttime protection had already pulled into place by the curb.

Maybe the policeman outside could protect her physically, but she was being worn down emotionally, as well. Trevor scrambled to make an excuse to be with her until she was on stronger footing. "I'll stay with you until your car gets here."

Her expression softened as gratitude

filled her voice. "That would be nice. I can fix you some dinner."

Trevor waved at the cop on duty as they walked past him and entered Valerie's house. The heaviness that pressed down her shoulders seemed to lift when Valerie saw Bethany. The little girl toddled toward her mother, arms lifted up.

Mrs. Witherspoon rose from the couch where she had been stacking blocks on the coffee table with Bethany. "She's always so glad to see you."

Valerie nestled close to Bethany as her tiny hands wrapped around her neck. As always, Lexi greeted Valerie by wagging her bobbed tail and licking her owner's hand.

"Poor dog slept most of the day," said Mrs. Witherspoon. "You were smart to bring her home."

Lexi resumed her post in the corner keeping watch, lifting her head slightly to each movement the people around her made. The dog had never greeted him when he had come into Valerie's place.

Though Lexi was not openly hostile toward him, she seemed to be reserving judgment on him for now.

Valerie thanked Mrs. Witherspoon. The older woman left after giving Valerie a hug.

She turned to face him. "I hope you like grilled chicken and a big salad because that's what is on the menu."

"Sounds great," said Trevor.

"Can you keep an eye on Bethany while I work in the kitchen?"

Trevor settled down on the couch. Lexi moved to her bed in the living room, which provided her a better angle to watch Trevor.

Valerie handed Bethany a cup with a lid before moving to the kitchen.

Trevor held up one of the blocks toward Bethany. "You want to play?" He stacked one block on top of the other. Bethany watched him for a moment before retreating to the dog bed where Lexi had settled. She used the dog as a back rest while she drank from her sippie cup.

A moment later, Valerie came into the living room and swept Bethany into her arms. As she made her way back to the kitchen, bouncing Bethany and singing to her, Lexi rose to her feet and followed them.

Trevor sat in the living room alone. He heard the back door slide open. Valerie must have stepped out to grill the chicken. He walked to the open door where Valerie had started the barbecue. Lexi and Bethany lingered on the patio. Bethany balanced against a lawn chair while Lexi sniffed the perimeter of the yard, her bobbed tail swinging like a metronome.

The Serpent had managed once to get into Valerie's yard; she might try again. He peered over her fence at the surrounding backyards.

After placing the chicken on the barbecue, she looked up at him. Weariness marked her features; her eyes lacked that sparkle that he loved. What he wouldn't give for the light to return to her eyes, to see her smile and hear her laughter.

As Valerie sat in the lawn chair and gathered Bethany into her arms, Lexi stopped her patrol and settled down on the patio beside them. Bethany crawled out of her lap, wrapped her arms around Lexi's thick neck and kissed her. Valerie leaned forward to stroke the dog's head. They had become a tight cohesive unit—Valerie, Bethany and Lexi. Each of them looking out for the other.

Neither one of them had said anything about the attempt on her life less than an hour ago. Yet that reality hung in the air like a thick fog.

If they could make it through this, there would come a time when Valerie's life was no longer in danger. Things would return to normal for her. She could take Bethany to the park without fear.

As he watched Valerie slip down to the patio to talk to Bethany and stroke Lexi's ears, he wondered if there was room in their world for him after she no longer needed his protection.

Even as Valerie rose to her feet to turn

the chicken, he sensed the chasm in his own heart. She deserved better than him. Someone who understood the meaning of happy family.

She touched his hand lightly on her way back to where Bethany was nestled against Lexi. He felt a stirring deep inside, an overwhelming longing stabbed at his gut. These three females had been what he had been searching for all his life, but was there room in their world for him?

SIXTEEN

Valerie awoke to the sound of her phone ringing beside her bed. Struggling to get past the fog of sleep, she flipped open her phone. "Hello." Her voice sounded like she'd been eating gravel. She cleared her throat.

"Valerie, it's Trevor. Looks like Baby-face is willing to squeal on Murke if he thinks it will reduce his own charges. He heard through the grapevine that Murke was eating at a truck stop outside of town last night. Maybe he'll come back." He paused. "Officer Worth and I are heading down there now to ask some questions and watch the place a while. I'll catch up with you at the station when you get on duty."

She looked at the clock. She had over two hours before she needed to be at the station. "Okay, sure."

"Have your nighttime protection follow you to the station. Let's not take any chances."

Valerie took in a deep breath. "Yes, I will." She pressed the phone against her ear. "Did any of the officers have any word on Arianna's whereabouts?"

"You know I would tell you the second I heard anything."

Her throat tightened as she fought back frustration. "I know." What if Arianna had left town and would never be caught? "Guess I was just looking for a little hope to hang on to that all of this will soon be over."

She said goodbye and hung up, rolling over on her side and pulling the covers up to her neck as she prayed for a sense of peace even though the Serpent was still not in custody.

Bethany slept on her belly in the crib. Her sweet face turned toward Valerie.

She'd gotten through the entire night without waking or fussing, a victory and a sign that she was adjusting to her new life. Lexi slept protectively beside Bethany's crib, a sure sign that Lexi had bonded with Bethany.

Valerie rose from bed, showered and dressed and was ready to go by the time Mrs. Witherspoon knocked on the door. Bethany was up and sitting on the couch with her sippie cup. She clutched her pink rabbit in the crook of her elbow.

Valerie kissed her soft head. "See you in a little while, my sweet princess."

The drive to the station was uneventful. She finished up paperwork from the day before and checked the clock. She couldn't wait any longer to go out on patrol. Her neighborhood needed her. Trevor would just have to catch up with her on the street.

Captain McNeal caught her on the way out the door. "Where's Agent Lewis this morning?"

"He had a lead on Murke he had to

take," Valerie said. "I think I'm ready to go back out on patrol."

Concern etched across McNeal's face.

"I'll be all right," she assured. "Lexi is coming with me. Trevor should be done shortly."

"There is a patrol car three blocks away from your regular beat following up some house burglaries. They're canvassing the neighborhood so they should be there for a couple of hours."

McNeal never stopped thinking about the safety of his officers. He was one of the reasons she was so proud to be on the Sagebrush force.

She knew McNeal had been torn up about not being able to protect his own father when Rio had been kidnapped. "How's your dad doing by the way?"

McNeal offered her a quick smile. "He's coming around since he woke up from his coma."

"That's good to hear." She headed out to her patrol car.

Not wanting to interrupt him if he was

on surveillance, Valerie texted Trevor, advising him of the neighborhood she'd be patrolling for the next few hours.

The day was sunny and clear as she parked her car and prepared to patrol on foot. She opened the back door for Lexi. The number of children playing on lawns suggested that it must be a school holiday.

Several children came up to greet her and pet Lexi. The dog relished the attention, her little bobbed tail vibrating at a furious rate. She'd taken Lexi for talks at the local schools and all the kids knew her. Lexi seemed more energetic, more like herself.

Jessie Lynn rode up on her bike, her light brown hair catching glints of sunlight. She'd attached metallic streamers to her handlebars. Several children rode behind her.

"Officer Salgado." She braked, her eyes wide with excitement.

"You got your bike looking pretty spiffy there, Jessie Lynn," Valerie said.

A second child, a boy of about six,

came up on a bike and stopped behind Jessie Lynn. Two more children stopped, as well. All of them looking up at Valerie.

"What's going on here, kids?"

Jessie Lynn, the official spokesperson for the group, gripped her handlebars. "Are you still looking for that police dog that was stolen?"

"You mean Rio?"

"We saw a dog just like him over by the old auto shop." The boy pointed over his shoulder.

"Yeah, it was a German shepherd," said another child.

All the children nodded in unison before a third one added, "It was all mean and scary-looking."

"It wasn't mean." Jessie Lynn put her hand on her hip. "We saw him from far away."

"Yeah, we saw him running," a chubby-cheeked little boy said.

"He was running toward the old auto repair place?"

"Like sniffing around it," another child piped in.

Valerie listened intently. Could this be Rio? "Was there a person with him?"

All the children shook their heads in unison.

"All by himself," added the chubby-cheeked boy.

"I'll check it out. Thanks, kids." Valerie jogged down the street with Lexi taking up the lead. The old auto shop building was one of the abandoned warehouses in the area where she and Trevor had first spotted Derek Murke.

So much had changed since that first morning. Trevor's aloofness because of her rookie status was no longer an issue. He seemed to respect the work Lexi did. Yet, there was still some part of Trevor that held back. She'd noticed it last night at dinner.

The bike convoy of children followed her to the end of the block.

As excited as the band of junior detectives were, she couldn't put them in any danger. "Why don't you kids wait here?" As if on cue, four sets of shoulders drooped and heads bent in disappointment. "I'll let you know if I find anything." She turned a corner and headed up the street.

Strange that Trevor hadn't called her yet in response to her text, or showed up. If Murke was going to show at that truck stop, he should have been there by now. Maybe Trevor and Jackson had caught up with him and he'd run again. She felt a twinge of regret at not being able to be there when Murke was finally apprehended.

She approached the warehouse with caution. The kids had said the dog was roaming free, but that didn't mean that some member of the syndicate wasn't close by. She radioed dispatch to let them know she might need assistance. If this dog was Rio, it was possible that he had served his purpose for the syndicate and had been turned loose.

She pulled her flashlight off her utility belt and entered the warehouse. The shell of an old truck—tires missing and doors torn off—rested in the middle of the concrete floor.

Lexi hadn't alerted to anything. If there was another dog in the proximity, she would have smelled it. Lexi licked her chops and whined when Valerie looked down at her.

"Nothing, huh?"

She walked the interior perimeter of the shop. There were plenty of busted-out windows and a back door where the dog the children had seen could have gotten out.

She stepped out into the sunlight. Her cell phone rang. She clicked it on, expecting it to be Trevor.

"Hello."

Silence on the other end of the line and then the line went dead. Valerie clicked through to see what number had dialed her. A sense of apprehension crept in when she saw that it was Mrs. Witherspoon's cell number.

She dialed the number, pressing the phone hard against her ear. It went immediately to message. Had something happened to Mrs. Witherspoon? She wasn't a young woman. What if she was having a heart attack and Bethany was alone in the house? Valerie quelled the rising panic with a deep breath.

She didn't know anything yet for sure. Even as she tried to convince herself that her fear was unwarranted, thoughts of the threat that had been made against Bethany only days ago overwhelmed her.

Lexi stirred at her feet and looked up at her.

The phone rang so suddenly, she nearly dropped it. She pressed the receive button expecting to hear Mrs. Witherspoon's chirpy voice.

"Valerie?"

Normally, Trevor's voice would have brought a sense of relief, but not this time.

"Oh, Trevor." She still couldn't let go of her fear.

"Listen, I don't think Murke is going to

show. I got your text. Where is your patrol car at right now?"

"I'm not too far from the warehouse district where we first saw Murke."

"Is everything okay? You sound upset."

Invisible weight pressed on her heart. "Trevor, 1…think I'm going to drive back home real quick." She wouldn't be able to let go of this distress until she saw that Bethany and Mrs. Witherspoon were safe and sound.

"What's going on?"

"It's just…I'm worried about Bethany. I need to check on her. It's probably nothing, but Mrs. Witherspoon called and hung up…and now she's not answering her phone at all."

"I'll meet you over there," Trevor said, concern saturating his voice.

"It might be nothing…" said Valerie.

"We can't take that kind of a chance with Bethany, can we?" Trevor said.

"No, we can't." She liked the way he used the word *we* and how willing he was to drop everything just to check on Bethany.

Valerie left the abandoned auto shop and stepped out onto the street. Lexi's ears perked up as her attention was drawn up the block. A black dog crawled out from underneath a pile of old tires and rubble.

To the trained eye, the dog was clearly not a German shepherd. But children eager to help her find Rio could have easily made such a mistake. The dog offered them a passing glance as it slinked away.

Valerie jogged back to the patrol car, stashed Lexi in the back and slid into the driver's seat. As she pulled away from the curb, she glanced in the rearview mirror at a woman pushing a baby carriage up the sidewalk. Anxiety twisted her stomach into knots.

The car gained speed and she prayed that Mrs. Witherspoon and her precious Bethany were okay.

Rising tension bunched the muscles at the back of Trevor's neck. Traffic moved at a snail's pace as the streets filled up with commuters. He never should have separated from Valerie. If he had just stayed with her, they could have gone back to her house together.

He and Jackson had staked out the truck stop for over three hours. The only good thing that had made the morning not a total waste of time was that one of the waitresses had remembered serving Murke the night before. If this was Murke's new favorite hangout, they'd catch up with him soon enough.

His thoughts drifted back to Valerie. While Lexi provided some protection, he didn't like the idea of her being in the patrol car alone after what had happened last night. The dog would be no help at all if someone decided to run Valerie off the road.

Three cars behind him, Jackson Worth sat in his patrol car with his dog Titan. He had offered to go with Trevor to check on Valerie and Bethany.

The cars came to a complete halt behind a red light. The traffic was so backed up in this part of town, it would be several light changes before he even got through the intersection.

Valerie had sounded so afraid over the phone. His longing to be with her and comfort her made him want to jump out of the car and run the rest of the way to her house.

He gripped the steering wheel. Of course that wasn't rational. Even with the cars moving as slowly as they were, he couldn't run the mile or so to her house faster than driving.

Trevor shook his head. He'd had lots of irrational thoughts like that in the days since he'd met Valerie.

He had always thought of himself as a guy with two feet planted solidly on the ground, a reasoned and dependable problem solver. Not so, when it came to Valerie.

He gripped the steering wheel with clammy palms. If anything had happened to Bethany...

Valerie hadn't said anything on the

phone, but when she had suggested that Mrs. Witherspoon might not be okay, the first thought he had was of the Serpent.

His stomach clenched.

He looked out the window at the clear blue sky. The concern could be over nothing, too. Maybe Mrs. Witherspoon had just dropped her phone and couldn't get to it.

He glared at the red light, willing it to change.

Valerie pulled up to the curb of her house and jumped out of the patrol car, opening the back door so Lexi could get out, as well. No strange cars were parked on the street. The neighborhood was quiet. Unlike the neighborhood she patrolled, this area of town had mostly working couples without children, and senior citizens.

Only the sound of sprinklers and a car pulling into Mrs. Witherspoon's apartment building parking lot disturbed the silence.

On her drive over, she had tried Mrs.

Witherspoon's phone number several more times. Each time the call went to message, the weight on her chest increased until she felt like she couldn't breathe at all.

Lexi's feet tapped on the sidewalk as they made their way toward her front door. Valerie twisted the doorknob and stepped inside.

"Hello, Mrs. Witherspoon? It's me, Valerie."

The ceiling fan twisted above her, making a slight whirring sound.

Valerie's throat constricted as her heartbeat drummed in her ears. "Mrs. Witherspoon?" Her voice cracked. "Beth—any?"

From this angle, it didn't look like anyone was in the kitchen. Still, the hair on the back of her neck stood up. Bethany's stroller was by the door. Mrs. Witherspoon hadn't stepped out with her.

She walked toward the sliding glass doors with Lexi trailing behind her. The dog stopped suddenly and made a noise that was somewhere between a whine and a growl.

Bethany's bottle was on the counter, and there was a pot on the stove with steam rising out of it. Valerie ran around the island. Mrs. Witherspoon lay crumbled on the floor, not moving. Had she had a heart attack?

As she kneeled to check for a pulse, Valerie's mind raced at lightning speed. Where was Bethany? Mrs. Witherspoon was alive but unresponsive.

Valerie rose to her feet, intending to look for Bethany. Her finger touched her shoulder mic as she prepared to call for an ambulance for Mrs. Witherspoon when she noticed the sliding glass door to the patio was open. Valerie commanded Lexi to search the yard. A woman stepped out from behind her patio curtains and slid it shut, trapping Lexi outside. The woman ran toward Valerie.

Valerie had only a second to register that it was Arianna holding a canister of something. The Serpent lifted her hand

and sprayed Valerie's face. The sting was instantaneous. Her nose and eyes felt like they were on fire.

She heard Lexi scratching frantically at the patio door. Her bark was muffled by the glass.

Unable to breathe and with limited vision, Valerie reached for her gun even as she reeled backward toward the island.

"Oh, no, you don't." Arianna grabbed her hand and twisted it, trying to pull the gun free.

Her eyelids felt like they had hot acid poured on them. She closed her eyes against the pain. She held on to the gun while Arianna clawed at her arm.

Arianna grabbed Valerie's shoulder mic, ripped it off and threw it against a wall.

Behind her, she could hear the pot boiling. She reached back for it and flung it toward where she thought Arianna was.

She was rewarded with a blood-curdling screech. Hot water sprayed across her arm, as well, and she let go of the gun involuntarily. She heard it hit the floor, but couldn't see where it landed.

As she struggled to orient herself with limited vision, Arianna grabbed her by the hair and dragged her across the room. Valerie tried to twist free. The swelling inside her mouth and nose made it hard to breathe. Arianna pushed Valerie to the floor and bound her hands and feet with what felt like a scarf. She could barely keep her eyes open from the pain.

As she listened to Lexi's frantic barks outside, Valerie's anger intensified. She could not give up. All she had to do was stay alive until Trevor got here.

"What have you done with Bethany?" Her voice didn't even sound like her, filled with agony and terror.

"The same thing I am going to do to you," Arianna retorted.

Terror collided with her resolve at every turn. She would not let herself think about what might have happened to Bethany. "They will catch you."

"Fires are accidents, my dear, and that

is what this is going to look like." Arianna spat out her words.

The Serpent's voice chilled Valerie to the bone. An image flashed through Valerie's head. Arianna had been wearing gloves when she stepped from behind the curtain. Even if anything from the fire survived, there would be no evidence that Arianna had ever been here. Valerie had been lured here. It was probably Arianna who had made the phone call after knocking out Mrs. Witherspoon.

Arianna patted Valerie's bound hands. "Don't worry. Those will come off once the fire gets going. We don't want any signs of foul play, and I have a way of making sure you don't escape the fire." When Arianna stood close, Valerie could see where the hot water had burned the Serpent's arm. Her shoulder was soaked with water, as well.

The Serpent's voice grew a bit more distant as her heels tapped back into the kitchen and Valerie could hear her moving around in that room. "Your foolish old housekeeper left the stove on and it caught on fire. You came home and tried to stop the fire, but were overcome by smoke inhalation."

In the living room, Valerie struggled to break free of her bindings. Her instinct was to close her eyes against the pain from the pepper spray, but she forced them open. Every time the Serpent turned her back or looked away she wiggled her feet, loosening the bindings.

Arianna poured oil on a dishrag, turned the flame up on the gas stove and set the rag beside it. Flames shot up from the stove.

"I have fellow officers coming."

"Sure you do." As the flames spread across the countertop, Arianna poured more oil and added newspapers and magazines to the growing fire.

"They will be here any minute," Valerie said.

Arianna cackled.

What was keeping Trevor and Jackson,

anyway? They should have been here by now. She had to hold on.

Though she held her feet together to make it look like she was still bound, all she had to do was slip out of the loose restraints. Her hands were tied more tightly behind her back. She pulled the fabric and twisted her hands to loosen the restraints.

Arianna retrieved her purse and pulled out a hypodermic needle.

Valerie had a feeling it contained the same drug that had been used on Lexi a few nights ago. If she was not able to move, it would indeed look like she had come through the door and been overcome by smoke inhalation. The flames on the countertop grew higher as the room filled with smoke.

Arianna moved toward her with the needle pointing straight up. Valerie could see her gun sitting on a chair by the island. The flames had engulfed most of the island as bits of burning debris fell to the floor.

On the other side of the island, Mrs.

Witherspoon coughed. Would she wake up in time?

Valerie's vision was still fuzzy as though petroleum jelly was smeared across her eyes. Arianna drew closer.

She had to wait for the exact moment to pounce on Arianna. Too soon, and the Serpent would have time to move away. Too late and the needle would be embedded in her flesh, poison sinking in and paralyzing her.

Still standing, Arianna lifted the needle. Valerie had expected her to kneel on the floor beside her. Valerie worked free of her loose bindings and scooted away as Arianna brought the needle down toward her shoulder.

She grabbed Arianna's foot, pulling her off balance. Arianna crashed to the floor, but didn't drop the needle. Arianna lunged toward Valerie, but she angled out of the way and scrambled across the floor toward the gun.

Though her eyes still stung, her vision started to clear.

Arianna grabbed her foot. The grip was like an iron claw around her ankle. Valerie flipped back over and kicked Arianna, landing a blow to her burned shoulder. Arianna let go of her. Valerie coughed from the accumulating smoke as she ran to grab the gun by the island. Mrs. Witherspoon groaned and coughed. She must be coming to.

Lexi howled at the sliding glass door.

Valerie wrapped her fingers around the gun. Arianna pounced on her. The gun flew out of her hand. The two women scrambled across the floor toward the gun.

A stack of magazines by the kitchen island caught fire. The smoke thickened.

Arianna retrieved the gun and jumped to her feet. She pointed the gun at Valerie, who was still on her knees.

"Fine. I'll shoot you if that's the way you want it." She lifted the gun and took aim.

Valerie's breath caught as she stared down the barrel of the gun. What would happen to Bethany if she wasn't around to take care of her? Where was she now?

Lord, keep her safe. Whatever happens to me, keep that little girl safe.

Arianna's lips curled into a sneer. She put her finger on the trigger.

Trevor burst through the door with Jackson on his heels. He fired two shots. Arianna slumped to the floor.

Jackson kneeled on the floor beside the dying woman. He leaned close to the Serpent while she whispered something to him. Her body went limp and motionless. He called for an ambulance and then grabbed a wool throw from the living room and began to swat at the fire.

Trevor gathered Valerie into his arms.

Valerie was shaking uncontrollably. She clung to Trevor while her heart pounded against her rib cage and her thoughts raced at lightning speed. "I need to find Bethany. I need to find my daughter."

Trevor let her go and rushed over to put the fire out. "Get out of the house."

Valerie stumbled toward the stairs. "I

have to find Bethany." She still couldn't see clearly. She reached out for the banister which guided her to the top of the stairs. She held a hand out and pushed open the door of her bedroom.

Bethany lay in her bed. As Valerie drew close, Bethany did not stir or cry out.

Valerie fell to her knees, weeping and shaking. She heard the shrill scream of ambulances and fire trucks growing louder.

SEVENTEEN

Though his first instinct was to follow Valerie up the stairs, Trevor helped Jackson subdue the flames that were spreading across the kitchen counter. His gut twisted from thinking about what might have happened to Bethany.

Arianna lay prone and lifeless on the floor. When Trevor came around the island, he saw Mrs. Witherspoon on the kitchen floor. He kneeled. The older woman still had a pulse. He lifted her up and carried her outside.

Lexi howled and barked, clawing at the door.

Trevor found himself longing to be with Valerie. Was Bethany upstairs? Was she safe or had the syndicate made good on their threat and harmed her? His heart ached over the possibility.

"We need to get everybody out of here." Jackson opened doors and windows as the ambulance and fire truck sirens wailed through the city, growing louder and closer.

Trevor raced up the stairs. He found Valerie on the floor of her bedroom clinging to Bethany. The little girl was motionless in her arms.

His chest squeezed tight. "Is she…?" He couldn't say the words, his throat tightened with pent-up anguish.

Valerie looked up at him. Her green eyes glazed with tears.

Bethany lifted her head off Valerie's shoulder and turned to look at Trevor.

"She's all right." Valerie's voice faltered. "She slept through the whole thing."

A flood of love and joy that he had never known before brought tears to Trevor's eyes. He wrapped Valerie and Bethany in his arms. They were safe.

He couldn't imagine life without the

two of them. He didn't know what he was to Valerie. His feelings for her were stronger than ever, but what did she think of him?

Valerie's eyes were swollen. He could see the effects of pepper spray.

"We need to get you ladies downstairs and outside until the smoke clears." He led the two of them downstairs.

When they got downstairs, Arianna's body was being loaded onto a stretcher.

Trevor helped Valerie over to the ambulance where Mrs. Witherspoon had come to. The older woman held an oxygen mask to her face and had a blanket around her shoulders. She greeted Bethany and Valerie with a fierce hug.

Valerie repeated over and over, "I'm so glad you're okay."

Trevor spoke to one of the EMTs. "Valerie was sprayed with pepper spray."

"The effects will wear off in about forty-five minutes." The EMT rose to his feet and opened a drawer in the back of the ambulance. "I have some drops to help cleanse your eyes."

He took the drops from the EMT. "Valerie, I got something for your eyes."

Valerie handed Bethany over to Mrs. Witherspoon and turned toward him. "Thank you. They're still stinging."

She tilted her head back. Standing close to her, he touched her cheek and put the drops in. She bent her head and blinked.

"Better?"

She nodded.

Lexi came bounding around the house. Someone must have let her out of the backyard. She ran past Trevor, not even seeing him.

As Valerie kneeled beside him and spoke soothingly to the dog, he realized that was the bottom line. Even if Bethany and Valerie would welcome him into their lives, the dog didn't totally trust him. Lexi would do the job she was trained to do, but she had not given any indication that she had bonded to Trevor. She tolerated his presence because she was such a well-behaved dog, but he was still an outsider to her.

Valerie stroked the dog's face and ears. "Poor girl, I know you wanted to help me." The dog licked Valerie's face.

Gradually, the crowd dispersed and the ambulance took Arianna's body away. The fire department allowed Valerie to return to her house to get a few things. They advised her to find somewhere else to live until the smoke damage could be taken care of.

"Why don't you stay with me tonight, dear?" Mrs. Witherspoon said.

"I think we will do that." She turned and looked at Trevor. "After that I can probably stay with my folks or one of my brothers since Arianna is no longer a threat." Her soft, sweet voice radiated gratitude. "Thanks for coming to my rescue."

"I just did what any officer would have done," Trevor said.

She linked her arm through his. "You saved my life."

"Trevor, why don't you come in and have something to eat with us?" Mrs. Witherspoon ushered him toward her apartment. "You all could probably use a little break."

Valerie pleaded with her eyes. "Stay a while."

Trevor shrugged. As much as he loved his work, he'd rather be with Valerie and Bethany any day.

As they walked back to Mrs. Witherspoon's apartment, there was something different in Valerie's demeanor. She seemed to hold her head a little higher as though a burden had been lifted off her shoulders. Her life was no longer in danger.

Though the need to catch Murke still loomed large, he felt a sense of relief, too. They spent the afternoon baking cookies with Stella and Bethany.

Trevor could have almost fooled himself into believing that they were an ordinary family spending the day together until his phone rang.

Trevor recognized McNeal's number.

The captain spoke in rapid-fire manner. "We just got a call. A man matching Murke's description has broken into a woman's house and is holding her hostage. The SWAT team is always deployed in a hostage situation, but you and Valerie should take the lead on this."

"We can do that," Trevor said. He got the address from McNeal and hung up. He summarized what McNeal had told him and then added, "You can go if you feel up to it. You've been through a lot today."

Valerie looked over at Mrs. Witherspoon who said, "You go. Do your job. I can watch Bethany."

Valerie's gaze was intense and unwavering. "You helped me take down the Serpent. I want to be the one who helps you get Murke."

In the short time they'd been working together, she'd changed a great deal from a rookie to a confident police officer.

There was no one else he would rather take this call with than her.

Lexi rose to her feet. "I think she's ready to go, too," Valerie said.

Trevor touched Valerie's arm. "Let's go get him."

Once they were in the patrol car and speeding across town, Valerie radioed in to dispatch for more details while Trevor drove.

"The woman has locked herself in the closet…and she told us she's three months pregnant." The female voice from dispatch offered the last little bit of information in a neutral tone.

Valerie's gaze flitted toward Trevor. A hostage situation was dangerous enough. Now there were two lives at risk.

Valerie swallowed to push down some of her anxiety and keyed the radio. "Does this hostage have a name?"

"Her name is Nicki. Nicki Johnson."

"Thanks. Keep us advised." Valerie put the radio back in its slot.

Trevor turned onto the street that led out of town to the Lost Woods where Nicki's apartment building was. "We'll just have to make sure Nicki and her baby get out unharmed."

Lexi paced in the backseat ready to go to work. Valerie felt a fluttering in her stomach, a mixture of excitement and fear. Beneath the surface emotion, there was a deeper resolve. They would get Murke this time and he wouldn't get away.

She clicked off the radio and looked over at Trevor, whose jaw had formed a hard line. "This is it. I can feel it."

"Me, too," Valerie said.

The address dispatch had given them was on the edge of the Lost Woods. A series of run-down two- and three-story apartments and box-like houses in need of paint jobs. "Lot of drug arrests in this part of town. I wonder why Murke is here?"

Trevor shook his head. "It's not too far from that truck stop we had staked out."

Up ahead, the SWAT team had moved

into place, taking cover behind cars and crouching by the building.

Trevor got out while Valerie opened the back door of the patrol car for Lexi. A man in a bulletproof vest walked toward them. "Second-floor apartment. We've evacuated the building. The woman is hiding in a closet and has turned off her phone. She doesn't want to risk Murke hearing her talk."

"Why is Murke up there?"

The sergeant shook his head. "All she was able to tell us was that she's pretty sure he is armed, and he's been screaming something about a code."

"A code?" Trevor shook his head. "Let's see if we can talk him out. He doesn't know we are here yet, right?"

The SWAT team leader nodded. "It's been about ten minutes since the woman made the call. It's only a matter of time before he figures out she's in the closet and breaks it down."

Valerie stepped forward. "How many points of entry do we have?"

"A back door with a fire escape and patio, a front door inside at the end of a hallway." The SWAT leader turned toward the apartment building. "And she was able to tell us that the closet is at the back of the house."

From what she had seen with Murke so far, he wasn't going to give up without a fight, and he'd run the first chance he got. What would he do if he was backed in a corner and couldn't escape? If he got to the hostage, he'd use her as a shield. "We've got to keep that hostage safe. I say we don't let him know the whole SWAT team is here. He'll panic and start shooting or worse. We got to get him separated from the hostage." Valerie squared her shoulders. "I'll go to the front door and see if I can keep him distracted. Agent Lewis can go in the back and be in position to take him down if needed."

Trevor's face shone with admiration for Valerie. "I think Officer Salgado has a good idea."

"We need some kind of wire so Trevor

and I can communicate. If it looks like Murke is going to harm Nicki, all bets are off. You guys can storm the place."

It took only a few minutes for the team to equip Valerie and Trevor with earpieces and bulletproof vests. As they walked toward the building with Lexi heeling beside her, Valerie's stomach knotted with anticipation.

When they reached the entrance, Trevor clasped her arm and turned her toward him. He drew her into a hug, stroking her hair and kissing the top of her head. "Stay safe."

"You, too," her voice welled with emotion. This might be the last time he held her. They could both die. She closed her eyes and pressed her ear close to his beating heart while his arms surrounded her.

After a long moment, Trevor pulled away and rested his hand on her cheek. "Let's do this." He stepped away and disappeared around the back of the apartment building.

Valerie pushed open the front entrance

where there was a series of mailboxes and doors for the main-floor apartments. Taking in a deep breath, she traversed the stairs with Lexi beside her to the second floor. She walked down a silent hallway, her footsteps barely audible on the worn carpet. When she came to apartment 210, she stared at the chipped and peeling green paint of the door.

Inside, she could hear Murke calling Arianna names and ranting about how she owed him big time.

She touched her earpiece. "Trevor, I'm at the door."

"I'm headed up the fire escape to the back door. Looks like there is a curtain across it, so Murke won't be able to see me even if it opens up directly into the living room." Trevor's breathing indicated that he was moving quickly.

Valerie closed her eyes and prayed as she raised her hand to knock on the door. *Oh, God, help me.*

She knocked three times and then pressed her back against the wall, raising her gun in case Murke decided to start shooting.

In her earpiece, she heard Trevor whisper, "I'm in place by the back door."

From inside, there was more banging and pounding and Murke screaming, "You better let me in or I'm going to shoot this door down! Tell me the code, Nicki."

Time was running out. Murke had figured out where Nicki was hiding. With her heart racing, Valerie knocked again, this time louder.

The silence that followed was disconcerting.

"Derek Murke?" She spoke in a loud, clear voice even though her legs were wobbly. "This is Officer Salgado from the Sagebrush PD."

"Officer Salgado." Murke's voice dripped with sarcasm.

Down the hallway, the rest of the SWAT team had moved into place. Murke's voice had sounded like he was still halfway across the room. She needed him right by the door, away from Nicki before she gave Trevor the okay to enter.

"Why don't you come with me now, and we can all walk out of here in one piece." Valerie gripped Lexi's leash a little tighter. The dog tilted her head as though to give her a vote of confidence.

There was a long silence and then Murke's voice seemed to be right against her ear, even though there was a door between them. "How did you know I was even here?"

Valerie cringed. Saying that Nicki had called them would put the hostage's life at risk. "A neighbor saw you walk into the building holding a gun."

She stepped away from the door, not wanting to risk Murke hearing her and spoke to Trevor. "He's by the door."

"I'm going in." Trevor's voice was steady and filled with determination. "Looks like there is a hallway before the living room but no closet door. It must be at the other end. Can't get to it without Murke seeing me."

Valerie wiped the perspiration off her forehead. Now all she had to do was keep Murke talking.

"So what do you say, Derek? Open the door and everyone here gets out alive."

She held her breath during the long silence. Had Murke gone back to the closet or heard Trevor entering?

"And I go to jail, right?" Murke's voice blasted through the thin wood of the door.

"I could put a good word in for you," Valerie said.

Several moments passed but all she could hear was the sound of Murke's heavy breathing.

She stepped away from the door and whispered. "Trevor, where are you?"

He spoke in such a soft whisper she could barely hear him. "In the hallway. I can hear Murke. I'm about to turn the corner. Keep him talking. Going dark. Don't want to be heard."

She turned back toward the door. "So what do you say, Derek? How about you unlock this door?"

Seconds ticked by. What was he doing in there?

"Derek?"

Nothing. No noise. No indication of a fight. Had Murke gone back to the closet where Nicki was? Had he figured out that Trevor was in the house? Certainly she would have heard the sound of a struggle.

Lexi looked up at Valerie, licking her chops.

She made a split-second decision, stepped away from the door and charged it, lifting her leg to break it down. The thin door crumpled like balsa wood. She took in the scene. Murke hiding behind a china hutch, Trevor turning the corner and looking at the door, where Murke should have been. Murke raising his gun. Lexi bounding across the carpet as a pistol shot shattered the silence.

Lexi yelped and fell to the floor, blood spreading across the carpet. Murke had shot the dog. Lexi had taken the bullet intended for Trevor.

"Drop the gun!" Trevor yelled. "Down on the ground."

Valerie moved in, her own gun drawn. "You heard him, hit the floor."

Lexi's anguished yelp pierced her heart, but she couldn't help her. Not yet. Not until Derek was no longer a threat.

Murke lifted his hand and let the gun fall. Valerie kicked it away so he couldn't pick it up again. The SWAT team swarmed in.

Trevor turned toward one of the SWAT team members. "Hostage is down that hall in the closet."

Valerie fell to the floor and wrapped her arms around Lexi. The dog licked her hand twice and then lost consciousness.

One of the SWAT team members escorted a slender woman with brown coppery hair into the living room.

Nicki swiped at her eyes that were red from crying. "He kept shouting about a code. He said Arianna told him I had the code."

"You know Arianna?" Trevor was already kneeling on the floor beside Valerie.

"Yes, she's my cousin." Nicki let out a cry when she saw the injured dog on the floor. She looked down at the dog, her voice filled with sympathy. "What happened?"

Valerie could feel herself shutting down, going numb. All she could think about was Lexi. Trevor's voice pulled her out of shock. "We need to get her to a vet."

More SWAT team members came into the house. Two of them had already gotten Murke to his feet and were leading him out.

Murke thrashed like an animal caught in a trap when he was led out. "That score should be mine. By rights that score should be mine."

Nicki had retreated to the kitchen and returned holding three clean white towels. "Here, for your dog." She kneeled beside Valerie and gazed at her with kind blue eyes.

Valerie placed the towels over the hole

where the bullet had gone in on Lexi's back flank. So much blood.

Trevor placed a hand on Valerie's shoulder. "We can get her to the vet's faster than they can get here."

Trevor gathered the Rottweiler into his arms. She looked so lifeless...like a rag doll. As he raced out of the apartment and down the hall, Valerie slipped past him. "I'll bring the car around."

Her feet pounded down the hallway. Inches felt like miles as she ran outside to the patrol car, praying that Lexi wouldn't die.

The lump in Trevor's throat made it hard to swallow. Lexi was warm against his chest as he ran down the stairs. This dog had saved his life. She wasn't going to die on his watch—not today, not any day.

Outside, the bright sun stunned him. He hadn't noticed what a beautiful day it was, not the kind of day you expect to lose a dog you've come to love. And she had proven that she loved him, enough to give her own life to protect him.

Valerie pulled up to the curb.

Still cradling Lexi, he got into the passenger side of the SUV. His shirt was covered in blood. The dog's rib cage still moved up and down, but her body was limp and lifeless.

Valerie sped away from the curb. "I've already called the vet. She's prepping the surgery room." She glanced from the dog to Trevor.

He wanted to offer her reassurances, but as he held Lexi, he wasn't so sure he could do that. She was barely hanging on. She'd lost a lot of blood. "It shouldn't take us long to get there." His voice was solemn.

Once she was away from the residential areas, Valerie accelerated. Plowed fields and then the trees of the Lost Woods clipped by.

Please, God, don't let this dog die, Trevor prayed.

Dr. Constance Mills was waiting for

them outside when they pulled up. "Let's get her inside. We're all ready for her."

Trevor carried Lexi into the operating room and laid her on the metal table. Two assistants went to work putting an IV in her leg while Dr. Mills assessed the wound. She spoke to one of the assistants. "We'll need a 7 mm trach tube and some lactated ringers."

Valerie shuddered and let out a gasp.

Dr. Mills looked up at her. "You should wait outside. Use my office, it's more private. You might be able to find a clean shirt."

Trevor glanced down at his own shirt. It was covered in blood. He felt as though he were walking under water as he pulled Valerie out of the operating room. He stood in the hallway for a long moment, not able to process what he needed to do next.

Valerie rubbed her temple. "Umm…I think her office must be this way." She stopped, bursting into tears. "What am

I going to do without her? What if she doesn't make it?"

Trevor gathered her into his arms. Anguish twisted inside him, made his throat tight. He couldn't speak. He held her until her crying subsided. He opened the door to the office where they found a T-shirt for Trevor with the name of the vet clinic on it and an operating smock for Valerie.

When Valerie looked down at her own bloody shirt, the tears started all over again. He held her again.

As he drew her close, he prayed.

"God, I don't know what your will is for Lexi, but we sure like having her around." His eyes grew moist. Life without Lexi… He didn't even want to think about it.

After several minutes, Valerie pulled away. She looked up at him with glazed eyes, still unable to say anything. He held her for a moment longer.

After they both had changed out of their bloody shirts, they stood in the hallway.

"I don't want to go back into the regular waiting room. Someone is bound to ask me what my pet is here for, and I just can't bear that kind of small talk." Valerie's voice was paper thin.

He led her out to the back exit of the clinic where horses trotted around a small corral. The sun warmed his skin.

Valerie looked up and stared at the sky, placing her hands over her face. "I need to see how Bethany is doing."

She pulled her phone off her belt and stepped away from him. He caught bits and pieces of the conversation. A desperation colored her words as she suggested that Stella bring Bethany to the vet clinic. Her eyes met Trevor's as she finished her sentence, "...so we can all be together."

Is that how she saw them now, as family that needed to be together during this uncertain time? She hung up the phone and offered him a faint smile. Her wide green eyes were filled with affection that drew him in.

He stepped toward her, ready to take her in his arms again. The moment was shattered by his phone ringing. He stepped away, a sheepish grin on his face. He looked at the number on the phone. "Sorry, it's Officer Worth. You might want to listen in, too."

He rested an arm on the corral as Valerie came and stood beside him, resting her hand on his shoulder and leaning close to him.

"Hello, Jackson. Valerie is here with me."

"Yeah, I heard about the dog. I hope she makes it," Jackson said.

Trevor swallowed hard. "Me, too."

"McNeal asked me to fill you guys in. They've got Murke down at the station." Murke hadn't escaped custody this time. And Trevor knew he would be put away for good. Finally, he had some justice for the death of Agent Cory Smith.

Jackson continued. "Since he's not talking, McNeal thinks we might have to bring the woman at the apartment in for questioning. This Nicki Johnson. She was related to the Serpent. She might know something."

"Yeah, we don't know what her level of involvement is. Derek seemed to think she had some sort of code that would help him with his big score, which has to be whatever it is the syndicate has been looking for in the Lost Woods. Arianna must have known something about it, and Murke must have coerced her into telling him that this Nicki person had it."

"That's what I wanted to talk to you about. When Arianna was dying, she whispered three words to me that make sense now," Jackson said.

"What did she say?"

"Cousin. Code. Danger."

"Sounds like the Serpent was having some last minute guilt pangs over sending Murke to terrorize her cousin," Trevor said.

"Maybe. Hard to say." Jackson seemed to be mulling all the information over and had fallen into a silence.

Trevor's own thoughts wandered again to the fate of the loyal dog lying on the operating table. "Listen, I got to go."

"A lot of people in the department are praying for Lexi," Jackson said. "I know I am."

Trevor hung up the phone and turned toward Valerie. "Did you get all that?"

She nodded. "I don't want to think about any of that right now." Anxiety showed itself in the deep furrows between her eyebrows. No doubt, her mind was on Lexi, too.

He brushed a strand of hair from her face. "Let's just walk." He took her hand and walked around the corral and into a field of bluebonnets. They walked without saying a word. There was nothing he could say to ease the fear. He felt it, too. That voice resonated deep inside of him.

What if Lexi didn't make it?

Twenty minutes later, Mrs. Witherspoon pulled up with Bethany. They ran to meet her in the parking lot of the vet clinic. Bethany's bright smile cheered him as Stella handed her over to Valerie. She offered Valerie a hug and kiss and a promise to keep praying for Lexi before driving away.

Bethany reached over and patted Trevor's cheek. As he leaned close to Valerie, their shoulders touching, he was overwhelmed with the love he felt for her and for Bethany.

He did love them both…and he loved that dog, whose life hung in the balance.

One of the assistants who had been with Dr. Mills opened the door to the vet clinic. "There you two are. You can come in and see Lexi now."

Valerie looked up. "Is she…?"

The assistant offered a quick smile that didn't quite reach her eyes. "I'll let the doctor explain."

Valerie tensed and looked up at Trevor. "Do you think we should take Bethany in the operating room?"

"I think we should all be together, whatever the news." He rubbed her back.

They stepped through the waiting room where a woman sat holding her cat and another woman sat beside a little girl who had a birdcage on her lap. A little yellow bird tweeted inside the birdcage. The cheerful tweeting of the bird stood in sharp contrast to the sense of dread he felt. What if they were being ushered into the operating room to say goodbye to Lexi?

They slipped inside the operating room where Lexi lay motionless on the table with a blanket over her. She had a breathing tube in her mouth. An IV stand was close to the operating table. The steady beep of the monitor indicated that Lexi had vital signs.

Dr. Mills looked like she had aged ten years. She leaned back against a cabinet filled with medicine.

"How does it look?" Valerie's voice wavered, fear evident in every syllable.

Dr. Mills pulled off the surgical cap and rubbed her eyes. "It was really touch and go. She lost a lot of blood at the outset. The muscle in her back leg is just torn to pieces. She's going to have a long recovery ahead of her."

Valerie let out a heavy breath. "But she'll make it." She handed Bethany over to Trevor and rushed to stroke Lexi's ears.

The doctor nodded. "She'll make it."

Bethany wrapped her arms around Trevor's neck as though it were the most natural thing in the world for him to hold her.

"I'll leave this little family alone with her for a minute." Dr Mills left, closing the door softly behind her.

Valerie spoke without taking her eyes off Lexi. "She thought we were a family."

Then she looked over at him, green eyes shining. He took in the wonder of holding Bethany, of having the little girl feel comforted in his arms. Trevor's heart pounded and in that moment, he knew what he needed to say. "That sounds like a pretty good idea to me."

She blinked, color rising up in her cheeks. "What are you talking about?"

Trevor moved around the operating table so he stood face to face with Valerie. "I would like for us to be a family."

Valerie rubbed Bethany's back. "Do you mean that?"

He nodded as joy welled up inside him.

Bethany patted his chest and made "Ba ba ba" sounds.

"All three of us?"

"All three of my girls." This is what he had been looking for most of his life…a family.

Her eyes were radiant with love. "Yes, I think we would like that."

Trevor brought Valerie into a hug with him and Bethany.

Lexi let out a faint whine and licked Valerie's hand. "I think she approves."

They laughed. Valerie tilted her head. He kissed the woman he wanted to spend the rest of his life with.

* * * * *

Dear Reader,

I hope you enjoyed reading about Lexi and seeing how K-9 police units help fight crime. After going for many years without a dog, we finally took the plunge two years ago and got a dog. His name is Bart and he is a spastic, nervous little border collie. We adopted him from a shelter. Bart and his mom were found abandoned in a rental home. We don't know if Bart had any brothers or sisters. Bart is not the dog I expected, but he is the dog I needed. My heart melted when, as a puppy, he sat at my feet and looked up at me as if to say, "What can I do for you?" He is super tuned in to the movements and emotions of each family member (after all, we are his sheep herd). He follows me from room to room. Don't get me wrong, intelligent dogs can also be stubborn dogs. When I command him to do something and he tilts his head, but doesn't move, I know full well he understands what I said and is choosing not to obey. We are still training him not to run up to the road and bark at passing bicyclists and walkers. Even with all that, I can't believe the level of joy and humor Bart has added to our lives. Though I grew up in the country with a dog always around, I defined myself as a cat person. I still love cats, but having Bart has made me a dog person, too. Just like Lexi in *Guard Duty,* I see how much Bart's loyalty, attentiveness and unconditional love has added to my life.

Sincerely,

Sharon Dunn

Questions for Discussion

1. Lexi is not only a trained police dog, but she is a loyal and loving pet. Have dogs been an important part of your life as a child or as an adult?

2. Why is Trevor hesitant to work with a rookie?

3. Valerie and Trevor have conflicting philosophies about what their role as law enforcement officers should be. What is the root of that conflict? Do you think it helps or hurts them in working together?

4. Trevor and Valerie have very different family backgrounds. What are some of the differences?

5. Do you think the differences will help or hurt them in their relationship?

6. Why is Trevor closed down to the idea

of getting married and having a family? What does he fear?

7. What was the most exciting scene for you? Why?

8. To keep her word to her sister, Valerie has chosen to raise Bethany, even though she feels ill equipped for the job. Have you ever had to undertake a task you weren't sure you could do?

9. What were the moments in the book when Valerie gained confidence as a mom?

10. Did you agree with Captain McNeal's decision for Valerie to go off active duty after there was an attempt on her life? How would you have handled that situation?

11. What evil desires motivated Derek Murke to do the things he did?

12. Do you think Valerie becomes a bet-

ter police officer by working with Trevor?

13. Other than Trevor and Valerie, who was your favorite character and why?

14. Why doesn't Valerie want to go to a safe house even though her life is under threat? What motivates her to want to stay on patrol?

15. What did you learn about K-9s and the work they do? Do you think they are a valuable asset to a police department?

ReaderService.com

Manage your account online!

- Review your order history
- Manage your payments
- Update your address

---

*We've designed
the Harlequin® Reader Service
website just for you.*

Enjoy all the features!

- Reader excerpts from any series
- Respond to mailings and
  special monthly offers
- Discover new series available to you
- Browse the Bonus Bucks catalogue
- Share your feedback

Visit us at:

ReaderService.com

RS13TR